FIZZOPOLIS
FLOOZOMBIES!

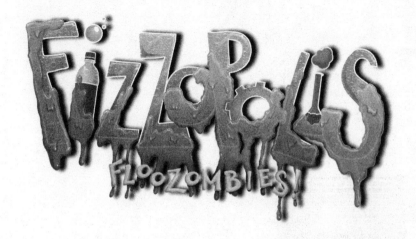

FIZZOPOLIS

FLOOZOMBIES!

PATRICK CARMAN

Illustrated by
BRIAN SHEESLEY

KATHERINE TEGEN BOOKS
An imprint of HarperCollins Publishers

Katherine Tegen Books is an imprint of
HarperCollins Publishers.

Fizzopolis: Floozombies!
Text copyright © 2016 by Patrick Carman
Illustrations copyright © 2016 by Brian Sheesley
www.harpercollinschildrens.com

Library of Congress Control Number: 2015952416
ISBN 978-0-06-239392-0

Typography by Joel Tippie
16 17 18 19 20   CG/RRDH   10 9 8 7 6 5 4 3 2 1

First Edition

For Karen, Sierra, and Reese—my three favorite girls
in the whole wide world
—P.C.

For Samanthaa and Jenna—my little angels
with Daddy's sense of humor. So proud . . .
—B.S.

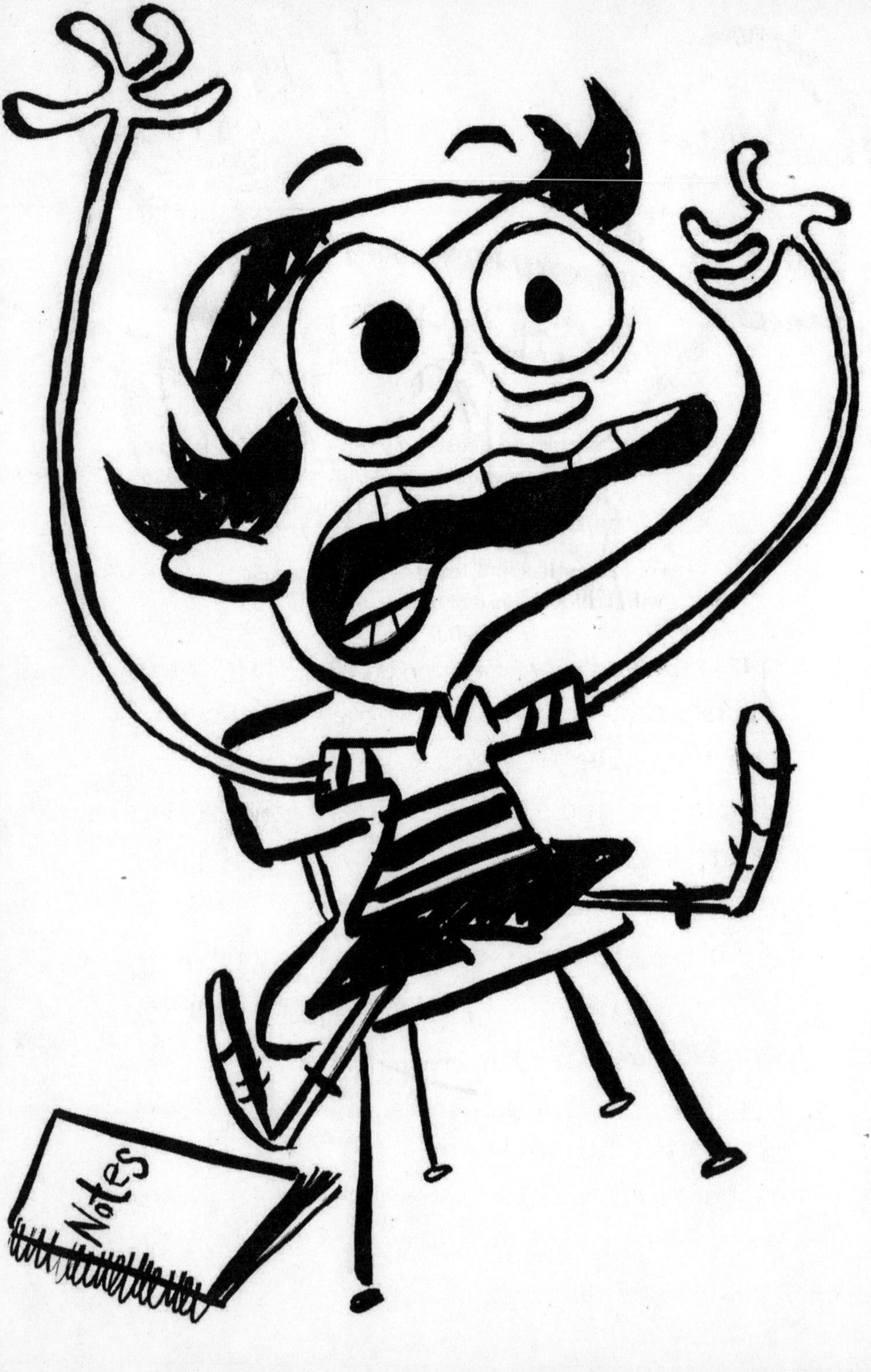
Notes

CHAPTER 1

I'm Harold Fuzzwonker and I'm sitting in my classroom where Miss Yoobler is about to start a movie. Miss Yoobler has terrible taste in movies, and she never gives out popcorn. And she makes us take notes! Who takes notes during a movie?

"Now, class," Miss Yoobler droned. "*The History of Flour* is an informative and exciting documentary that will change the way you think about hot dog buns and pizza crust. Prepare to be moved."

The History of Flour was part four of a series

we were watching. These movies make me feel like my eyeballs are going to fall out and roll around like marbles on the classroom floor. We've already completed *The Story of a Chicken*, *Butter My Toast*, and *Super Cobs: The Amazing Journey of Corn*.

Miss Yoobler turned off the lights and started the movie. The screen filled with rows of swaying wheat and the sound of a tractor.

My best friend, Sammy, leaned slightly toward me and said, "I thought this movie was about pizza."

"And hot dogs," I added.

"You two are total airheads," Jeff Flasky said. Flasky had an enormous head and big, round eyes. He was also the smartest kid in class.

"What does a field full of whatever that

2

stuff is have to do with pepperoni pizza?" Sammy wondered. Flasky rolled his eyes as Miss Yoobler took three long strides toward us.

"Zip it, Fuzzwonker," Miss Yoobler said. She was the strictest teacher in the entire United States of America. Unfortunately, Sammy was in a talkative mood and she kept yammering about pizza and hot dogs. Miss Yoobler took three more steps and loomed over my left shoulder like Frankenstein.

Garvin Snood was sitting two desks over. He was always trying to figure out the secret of Fuzzwonker Fizz, so we had to be extra-super careful around him.

"You boneheads are in for it now," Garvin sniggered. He laughed like a hyena.

Miss Yoobler tapped her foot on the linoleum. It was like Chinese water torture.

"Harold Fuzzwonker, come with me," she finally said.

"Take me!" Sammy said. "I'll gladly go to the principal's office!

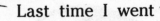

Last time I went there they had donuts and better movies."

I picked up my backpack and Miss Yoobler marched me to an empty desk in the farthest back corner of the class. Sammy waved at me with a faraway look like we were separated by a giant river filled with crocodiles.

"Let's see if sitting in Siberia will help you concentrate, Mr. Fuzzwonker," Miss Yoobler said. She stood next to me for a while, but then Garvin Snood threw a wad of paper at Jeff Flasky and hit him in the side of his huge head.

"Garvin!" Miss Yoobler yelled, and then she was on the move toward Garvin's desk.

I looked down at my backpack sitting on the floor. It was squirming wildly like a tennis ball was bouncing around inside. There were also muffled noises coming from under the flap.

"Oh, great," I said. I nudged the side of the bag with my foot and made a *shhhhhhhh* sound. For a second everything was calm, but then the whole bag rolled over on its side

HA HA HA HA HA HA HA HA HA HA HA HA HA HA HA HA HA HA HA HA HA HA HA HA HA HA HA HA HA HA HA HA

and flopped forward. I heard the sound of laughing in there. I grabbed my backpack and hauled it under my desk before it could flop and roll any farther away.

"Calm down, little buddy!" I whispered. "I'm already in enough trouble as it is."

In case you don't know about my best good buddy who lives in my backpack, his name is Floyd. How he got there takes a little explaining, but since we're watching a mindless movie about flour, I can take a second to fill you in.

The super-short story of how Floyd got in my backpack, by me, Harold Fuzz-wonker (sure to be more interesting than The History of Flour):

My dad is Dr. Fuzzwonker, and he keeps a top secret laboratory under our house. It's the biggest laboratory you've ever seen—like several football fields—because some of what my dad makes needs a lot of space to roam. He creates Fuzzwonker Fizz, the soda pop that produces the biggest burps in the world. It's extremely popular stuff that comes in about one hundred flavors. You should try some!

Classroom status update: I need to speed this up because Floyd is sucker punching me in the solar plexus. Ouch. I advise reading the next paragraph at double speed!

Dr. Fuzzwonker uses a machine he calls the Fizzomatic to make Fuzzwonker Fizz, but he also used it to make Floyd. Floyd is a Fizzy, and he's not the only one. There are at least a hundred different Fizzies in my dad's humongous secret space under the house, which is probably why he calls it Fizzopolis. Floyd just happens to be the smallest one and the biggest troublemaker.

AHAHA

And that's why he has to go with me in my backpack to school. If he stays in Fizzopolis without me, he misses me too much and that makes him go bonkers. He makes huge messes and causes colossal problems. So every day when I leave for school I carefully pack Floyd into my backpack and hope he stays quiet. This almost never happens, so I spend a lot of time struggling to keep Floyd a secret.

See how short that was! And trust me, you didn't miss anything important about flour. You're all good. I can't say the same for myself. While you've been busy reading all about Floyd, I've been freaking out.

My backpack was flopping toward the front of the class like a sack of potatoes rolling down a hill.

I couldn't yell at Floyd or everyone would hear me and ask me who Floyd is. I glanced toward the door, where Miss Yoobler had stationed herself. At first I thought she's staring down into her phone, probably texting some pro wrestler for advice about how to keep her class from disobeying her. But then I realize she's fallen asleep and that gives me some extra courage.

I got down on all fours and started crawling as the bag moved forward, closer and closer to the front of the class.

I passed a couple of other kids who were sound asleep, and then Jeff Flasky, who was diligently taking notes. The next desk I was going to pass would be Garvin's. Total disaster dead ahead.

The bag was getting dangerously close to

Garvin's mondo-sized foot, so I pulled a pencil out from behind my ear and threw it tomahawk-style at the back of Sammy's head. Luckily, it hit her noggin eraser end first. Sammy is my super-duper palamino. She's the only other kid in the world that knows about Floyd.

Sammy turned in Garvin's direction and narrowed her eyes like a ninja ready to strike. But then she saw me, and I nodded toward the bag creeping across the floor. Her eyes darted from me to the backpack moving on its own, nearly at Garvin's feet. Then she stared at Garvin.

"What are you looking at, weirdo?" Garvin asked.

Sammy sprang into action. In a matter of less than 1.3 seconds, she did five things in rapid succession:

She reached into her own backpack, pulled out a bologna sandwich, and took it out of the Ziploc bag.

She jumped into the air and did a roundhouse kick that landed squarely on my backpack! The bag (and Floyd inside) slammed into my

face and knocked me onto my back. Boy, she
could really kick hard. When I sat up, I had my
bag (and Floyd) in a bear hug.

When Sammy landed, she stared at Garvin
like she was going to hurl. Garvin had a look
on his face that screamed: *This kid is about to
barf on me!*

Sammy made a really loud BLAAAAAA-
GGGAAAAK sound and acted like she was
throwing up all over Garvin.

She tossed her bologna sandwich at him

and it bounced off his massive forehead. All the bread and bologna and lettuce came apart on his desk.

"AAAAAAAAAAAAAAUUAAAAAAU-UUAAAAUUUUAAAAA!" Garvin screamed. He was sure he'd been thrown up on and *wow* was he freaking out about it. It didn't look like real barf. It looked like a bologna sandwich.

"Garvin stole my lunch!" Sammy yelled.

"Sammy barfed on me!" Garvin yelled.

The whole class went bananas.

There was a lot of laughing and shouting and running around the room.

"Order! Order, I say!" Miss Yoobler said. She stomped over to Garvin's desk like an army sergeant. While all the chaos was going on in the room, I crawled back to my desk in Siberia and tied a bunch of knots on the bag flap so Floyd couldn't escape, then I slung the pack on and cinched it down tight in case it tried to roll away again.

"She threw up on me!" Garvin said from the other end of the room. "On purpose!"

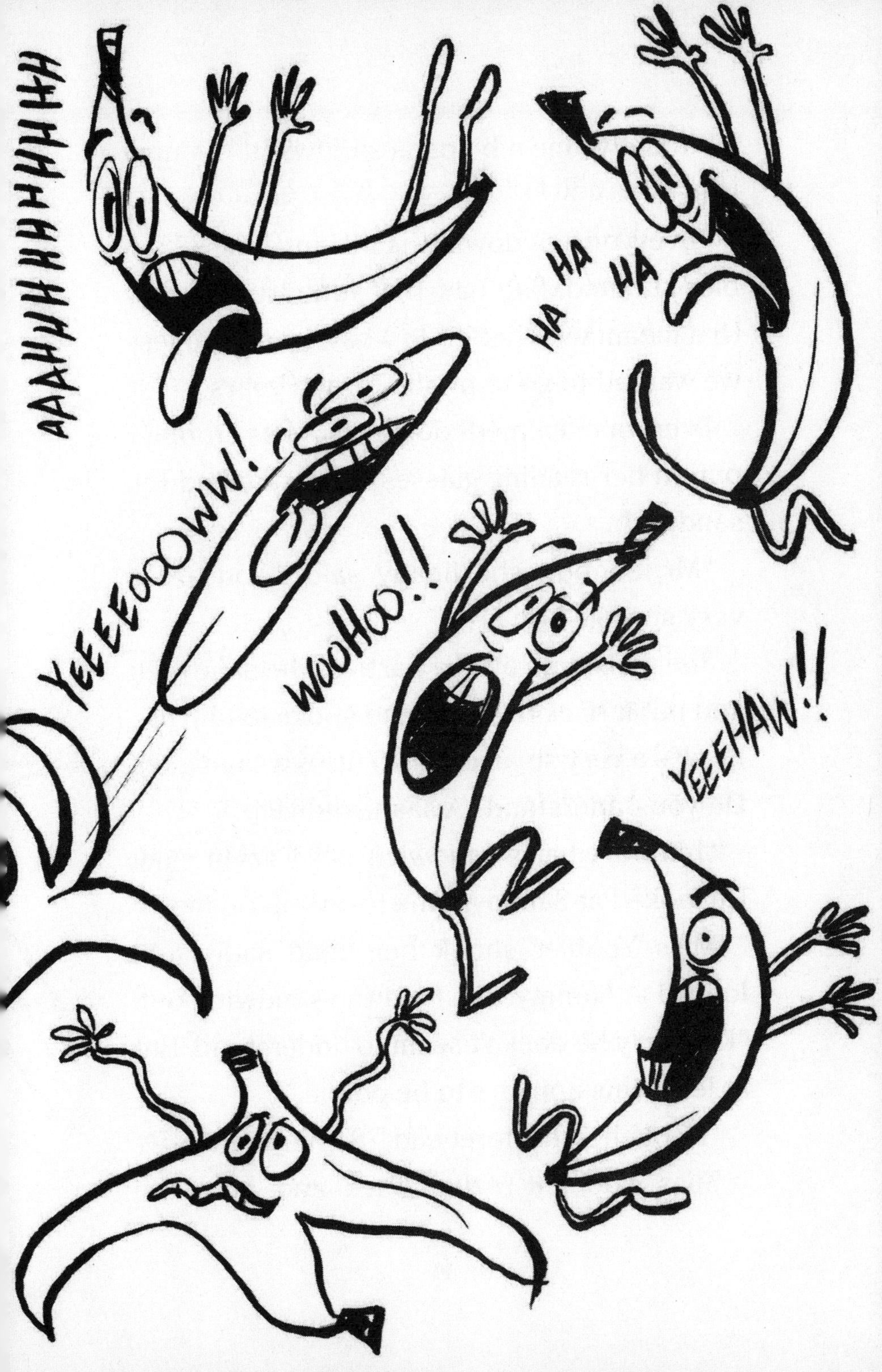

AAAHHHHHHHHHHHHHHH
YEEEEOOOWW!
HA HA HA
WOOHOO!!
YEEEHAW!!

"You owe me a bologna sandwich!" Sammy said.

"Everyone sit down this instant!" Miss Yoobler shouted. She had that tone we all knew that meant we'd better do what she said unless we wanted to go to prison for ten years.

Everyone calmed down as Miss Yoobler put on her reading glasses and examined the sandwich.

"Mr. Snood," she finally said. "You are a very strange boy."

She picked up all the parts of the sandwich and put it back together and spoke to him like he was a very small child. "This is a sandwich. Do you understand? A saaaaandwich."

"I know what a sandwich is!" Garvin said. He looked at Sammy. "She threw up on me!"

Miss Yoobler shook her head sadly and looked at Sammy. She held the sandwich out. "I'm sorry he doesn't seem to understand. But at least this appears to be edible."

"It touched his forehead," Sammy said.

Miss Yoobler reeled back and held the

sandwich as far away from herself as she could. She marched over to the garbage can and dropped it inside.

The class settled down and we returned to watching *The History of Flour.*

Floyd started bashing into me from inside my backpack. It felt like he was doing barrel rolls into my rib cage, so I squashed him against the back of my seat.

When school finally let out, Sammy and I ran to our bikes. We had to get out of there fast and figure out what the heck was going on with my best good buddy.

"Where to?" Sammy asked as we started off.

There was only one place where

we could safely let Floyd out into the open. It was a place where no one from the outside world would see him.

"Fizzopolis!" I said, and we tore off into the neighborhood at triple speed.

CHAPTER 2

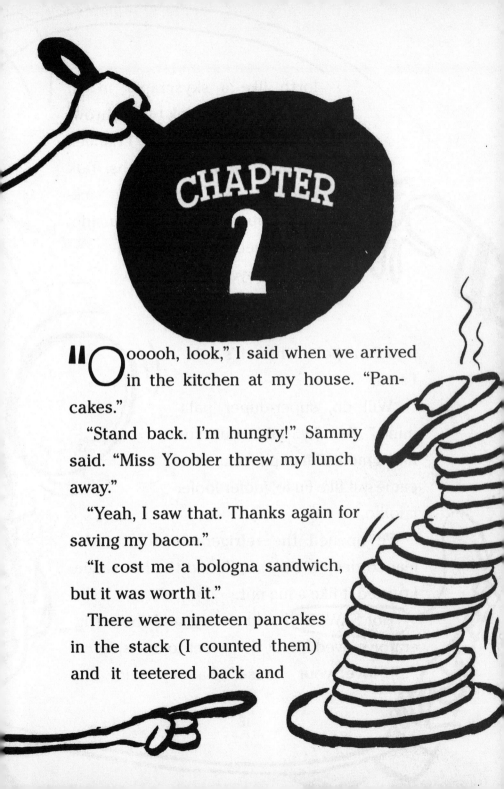

"Oooooh, look," I said when we arrived in the kitchen at my house. "Pancakes."

"Stand back. I'm hungry!" Sammy said. "Miss Yoobler threw my lunch away."

"Yeah, I saw that. Thanks again for saving my bacon."

"It cost me a bologna sandwich, but it was worth it."

There were nineteen pancakes in the stack (I counted them) and it teetered back and forth like a skyscraper in an earthquake. We took turns throwing them at each other like Frisbees and catching them in our mouths. Talk about a good time. I opened my backpack and dropped the last five inside, then cinched it tight again before Floyd could climb out.

"Come on, let's get into Fizzopolis where it's safe," I said.

"Will do, super-duper palamino," Sammy said. But she had a mouthful of pancake, so it came out like Fu fo, foofer foofer fafofifo.

We opened the refrigerator door and I leaned deep inside and found the hot sauce. I turned it like a lug nut.

"Hot SAWCE," I said slowly, and the refrigerator moved about three feet to one side.

"I love your house," Sammy said. She

reached down and picked up a nickel covered in dust bunnies and handed it to me.

"Thanks, I was looking for that," I said, and pushed a button on the wall.

"Remember the most important rule of Fizzopolis?" I asked.

Sammy nodded as the elevator doors opened.

"Don't tell anyone about all the cool stuff down there," Sammy said. "Got it!"

I handed Sammy a huge stick of bubble gum and put another stick in my mouth. We chewed and chewed until the gum was nice and gooey and then we threw both wads into the elevator. They hit the floor with a slobbery slap. We jumped into the elevator and made sure to land with one shoe each on a wad of gum, so

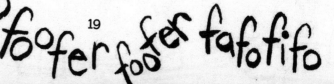

we were good and stuck.

"Here we go!" I said, and I pressed the button for Fizzopolis.

It felt like I was skydiving without a parachute as we plummeted underground.

"I can't get enough of this elevator!" Sammy said. But then our feet slipped out of our shoes and we spent the rest of the trip stuck to the ceiling. Both of us tried to crawl down the side of the wall but only made it halfway before the elevator stopped. We fell face-first on the floor and lay there like two bags of rice.

"Note to self," Sammy said as she sat up. "Always tighten laces before entering Fizzy elevator."

"I feel like we've covered this a thousand times," I said.

"Or two thousand," Sammy said. "We've definitely covered it."

"Always tie shoes super tight," I said as we put our shoes back on and yanked them off the gum stuck to the floor. "Come on, let's go find my dad."

We started off through the vast expanse of Fizzopolis. There are giant looping trees everywhere. They're purple and blue and green, and they rise hundreds of feet toward the high ceiling. There are caves and rock formations and a twisty-turny lagoon. There are conveyor belts by the hundreds, moving bottles of Fuzzwonker Fizz from place to place, and the gigantic Fizzomatic machine sits right in the middle of everything.

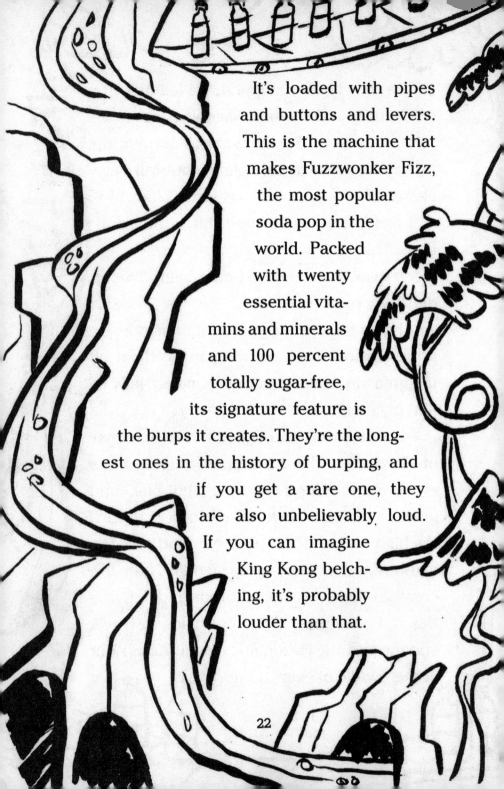

It's loaded with pipes and buttons and levers. This is the machine that makes Fuzzwonker Fizz, the most popular soda pop in the world. Packed with twenty essential vitamins and minerals and 100 percent totally sugar-free, its signature feature is the burps it creates. They're the longest ones in the history of burping, and if you get a rare one, they are also unbelievably loud. If you can imagine King Kong belching, it's probably louder than that.

And like I said earlier, the other thing the Fizzomatic machine makes is Fizzies.

"Hi, Franny," I said as we walked past the lagoon. "How's the cleanup going today?"

Franny is one of the many Fizzies in Fizzopolis. She has a hose for a nose so she can suck up water from the lagoon. Franny made a whole bunch of watery snarfing noises.

BUUUUURRRRRP!

"Sounds like it's going great," Sammy said. I thought so too, since Franny was making happy sounds. She went back to work and we kept walking.

We walked past more caves and trees and a Ping-Pong table. We said hi to a big yellow glob named George, and passed by Kevin, Stacy, and Phil—three more Fizzies who were too busy working to talk. All the Fizzies are different colors and if you pet them they crackle like their fur is carbonated.

There were Fizzies all over the place doing important Fizzopolis work like making sure

the bottles got labeled correctly. They made sure if you purchased a bottle of Lucy Lemon flavor you didn't end up with Larry Lime instead. Without the Fizzies to help get all the work done, there's no way my dad could keep up with the skyrocketing demand for Fuzzwonker Fizz.

"I'm surprised Floyd hasn't bugged me to use the bathroom," I said as we stared up at my dad's tree house laboratory.

Sammy leaned close to my backpack and listened. "He's making a lot of weird noises in there. Should we check on him?"

"You're right," I agreed, peeling off my backpack and setting it on the ground. "Better if Floyd freaks out down here than up there."

I undid all the knots I'd tied in the strings holding the flap shut. There were at least ten, so it took a while.

"Better stand back," I said. "He's been in there a long time. He might go a little wacky."

Sammy took two steps back as Floyd's green head popped out. He had a rascally look on

his face, never a good sign.

"Hey, little buddy," I said. "What was all that about at school? You almost got me in big trouble."

Floyd's eyes darted back and forth like he was thinking about making a run for it.

"What are you hiding in there?" I asked.

Floyd spoke just loud enough for me to hear him. "Who, me?"

I tried to peek around him into my backpack, but he kept moving to block my view. "Come on, Floyd. What have you got in there?"

Floyd launched into the air three feet over our heads. He did two and a half somersaults

and one twist in the pike position like he was in a springboard diving competition, and my bag was a swimming pool. He landed inside with a thud.

"He's weird," Sammy said.

Both Sammy and I leaned over and looked into the backpack. It was a tight fit for two of us, and we bonked heads. If Floyd tried to jump out of the bag again, he'd have to go through our faces. Double ouch.

"He's trying to hide stuff," Sammy said.

She was right. Floyd was pushing all sorts of things behind my binder and my calculator. It was dark inside the backpack, but it was obvious Floyd was up to no good.

"Come clean, Floyd," I said in my most serious voice.

Floyd got all bashful and stared at his belly button. He stepped away from the corner of my binder and pushed it aside.

"Uh-oh," Sammy said.

"No kidding," I agreed.

There was something in my bag that absolutely-positively-for-sure-without-a-doubt should not have been in there.

CHAPTER 3

"**Y**ou brought another Fizzy to school!" I said. "How could you?"

A tiny little Fizzy had walked out from behind my calculator. He was the size of a cockroach and looked like one too, only he stood upright on three legs. He was purple, he was furry, and he was trouble.

"Of all the Fizzies you could have brought to school, you brought him?" I asked.

Floyd opened his mouth to say something but stopped, scratching his head like he was still trying to determine how to get out of trouble.

"What do you have to say for yourself?" I asked in my best Miss Yoobler voice.

Sammy thought I was talking to her. "The acoustics in here are really good," she said. She practically had her whole head inside my backpack. Actually, so did I. It's a big backpack. Also stretchy.

Sammy was right: The sound inside my backpack was surprisingly awesome. It was like a concert hall.

"You know Floyd's travel buddy?" Sammy asked. She turned in my direction and her nose got squashed against the side of my head.

"Sammy, meet Grabstack," I said.

Grabstack was a total blowhard who thought he was a theater director. He was always putting on plays in Fizzopolis, usually of the Shakespeare variety. Grabstack was incredibly demanding with his actors. Somehow he'd acquired a British accent, probably from watching soap operas Dr. Fuzzwonker wired in from London.

"Why are people in my theater?" Grabstack said in his squeaky little British voice. "We're not even in previews yet! Get them out of here!"

Floyd looked up at me bashfully. "We're in rehearsals. It's a closed set."

"This is outrageous," I complained. "Who else have you got in there?"

Grabstack turned his nose up at Sammy and me. "They don't appreciate the theater. They're barbarians."

Floyd whispered something to Grabstack that made him roll his eyes.

"Oh, all right," Grabstack agreed. "If it will clear the theater, I'll introduce the cast."

Grabstack pushed my calculator so it lay flat on the bottom of my bag and one by one he introduced everyone who was sitting on it.

"We are bringing an enthralling adventure to life," Grabstack said. "It's my first original production, starring Mr. Pencil."

"Hey, that's my pencil," I said. Mr. Pencil rolled forward.

"And here we have Dime and Penny," Grab-stack continued. "Also Miss Ball of Rubber Bands, and the evil Mr. Lint Ball."

The dime and the penny and the rubber band ball and the lint just sat there.

"And the star of our show, the Floozemeister!" Grabstack yelled at the top of his lungs. He held out a wad of Snood's Flooze, the yuckiest candy in the world. It was made at the Snood Candy Factory by Garvin Snood's dad. The glob of Flooze had two eyes that were made of pebbles. It looked like a tiny bald head.

"I love this play," Sammy said. "They can really act."

"At last! Someone with real taste around here," Grabstack said. "She can stay."

Floyd held out his hand. "This is Wrinkles, who used to be a grape," he said.

"Floyd, that's a raisin," I explained. "And this play involving all the junk in my backpack cannot go on. At least not while we're at school."

"Off with his head!" Grabstack yelled.

"Wow, he really is a feisty little Fizzy," Sammy said.

"You have no idea," I said. "He puts on weird plays in Fizzopolis all the time. What an egomaniac."

"If you're going to insult me, please take your heads somewhere else," Grabstack said. "We have important work to do."

I looked at my best good buddy and I could tell he was in over his head. I felt sorry for Floyd, so I offered him a deal.

"You guys can practice in here all you want, but when we go to school you can't bring Grabstack with you. It's too dangerous."

Floyd and Grabstack had an epic Fizzy argument, so I pulled my head out of the backpack to get some fresh air.

"This might take a while," Sammy said as she stood up.

When we both turned around, a crowd had gathered. There were several Fizzies taking their lunch break.

"I think they're waiting for the show to start," Sammy said. All the Fizzies nodded while they ate their sandwiches. There were green Fizzies and blue Fizzies and one covered in stripes.

We waited as Floyd and Grabstack argued. And argued. And argued.

Finally, after about a million years,

Grabstack popped out of the bag and stood holding the Floozemeister in one three-fingered hand.

"If I can't lead this play at the Floyd Theater, no one can!" he blathered.

"It's not a theater," I said. "It's my backpack!"

Grabstack turned in the direction of the Fizzomatic machine and threw the glob of Flooze as hard as he could. The Floozemeister flew across the great expanse of Fizzopolis, bounced three times, and landed on the ground next to one of the giant Fizzomatic tubes.

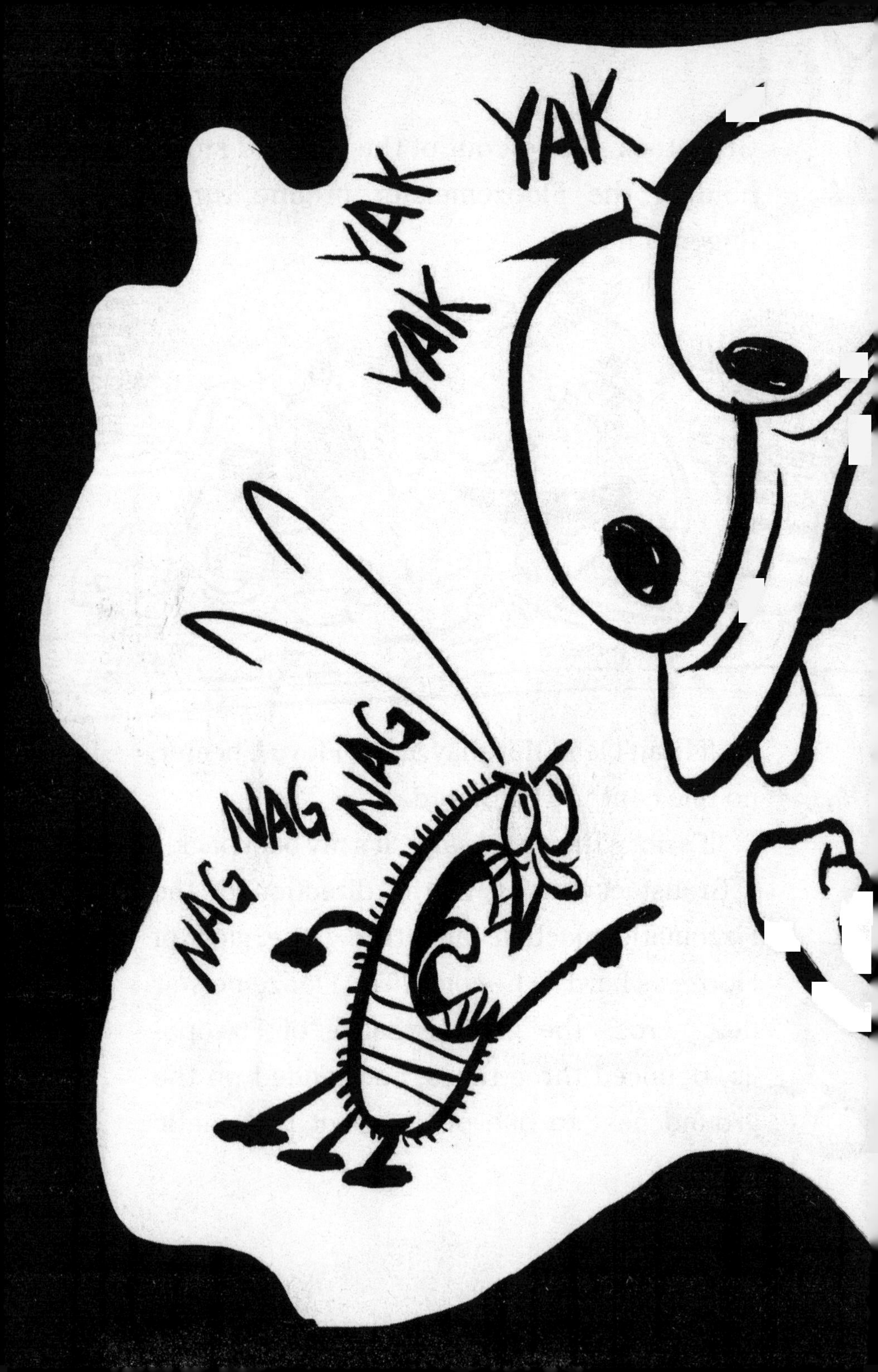
YAK YAK YAK YAK
NAG NAG NAG

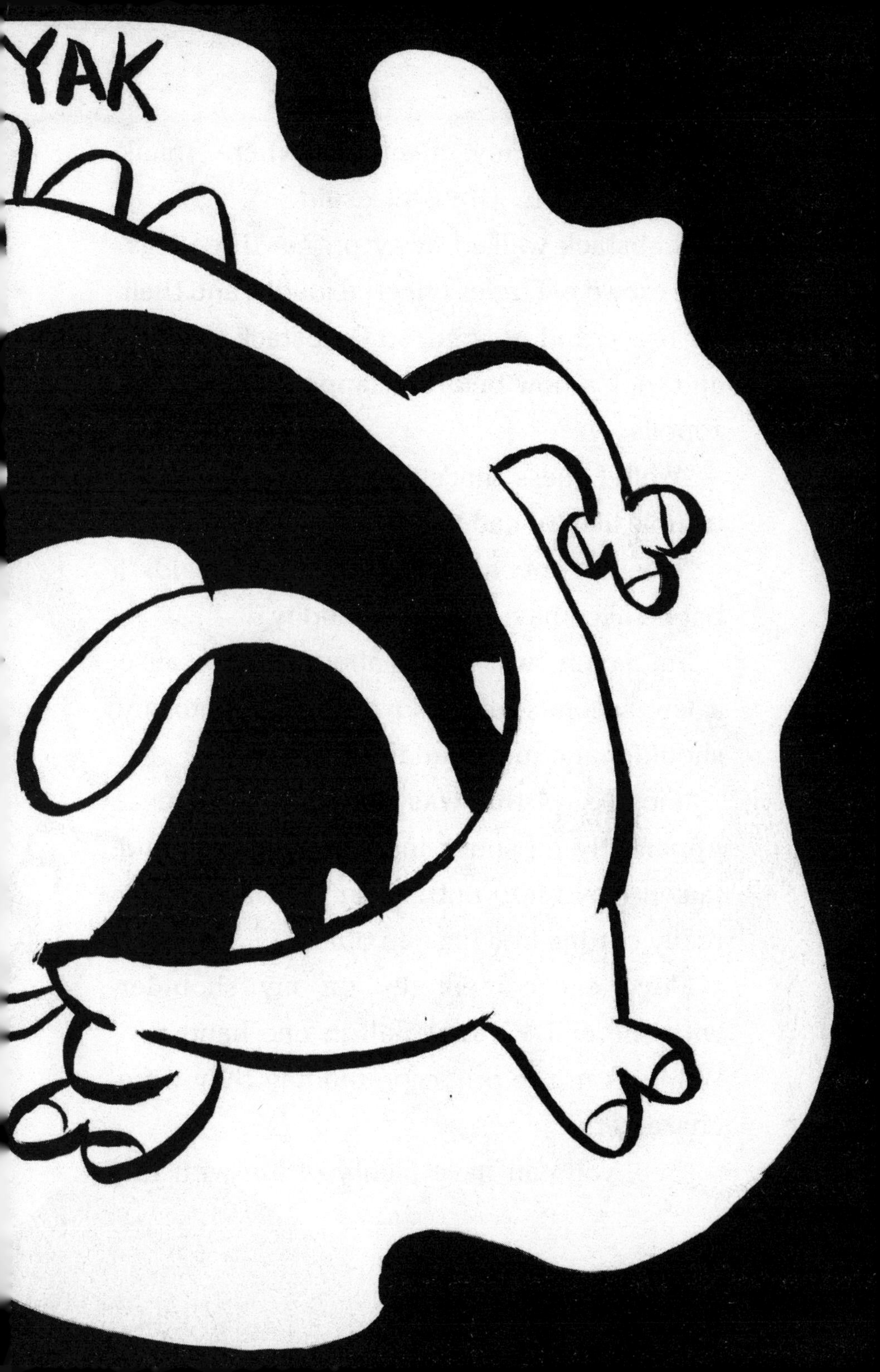
YAK

"I shall take my talents elsewhere, thank you very much," Grabstack said.

Grabstack walked away on his three legs. The crowd of Fizzies cheered loudly, and their fur fizzed and popped, so Grabstack stopped and took a bow before disappearing into Fizzopolis.

"Well, I guess that's that," I said. "No more trouble like we had today at school."

"I feel sort of bad for Floyd," Sammy said. "I bet he liked having a travel buddy."

But Sammy was wrong about that, because a few seconds later Floyd jumped onto my shoulder and mumbled into my ear.

"Floyd says this was all Grabstack's idea. Apparently he snuck into my backpack and talked Floyd into putting on the play. It was really cutting into his nap time."

Floyd sat contentedly on my shoulder with the evil Mr. Lint Ball in one hand and Wrinkles in the other, pretending they were characters.

"See, you can have plenty of fun with the

stuff in my backpack without Grabstack bossing you around."

Floyd nodded happily.

"Hang on," Sammy said. "I'll get Dime and Penny!"

The three of us put on a play while the Fizzies watched. Boy, was that fun. The evil Mr. Lint Ball was banished to the Fizzy forest in the end and all the Fizzies in Fizzopolis fizzed and popped and cheered.

We decided there was no reason to find my dad and went to work doing the normal chores we had in Fizzopolis. But while we were busy watching the Fizzy babies in the Fizzopolis nursery and helping Franny clean the lagoon, someone else was causing trouble.

Grabstack was planning something that could mean big trouble in Fizzopolis!

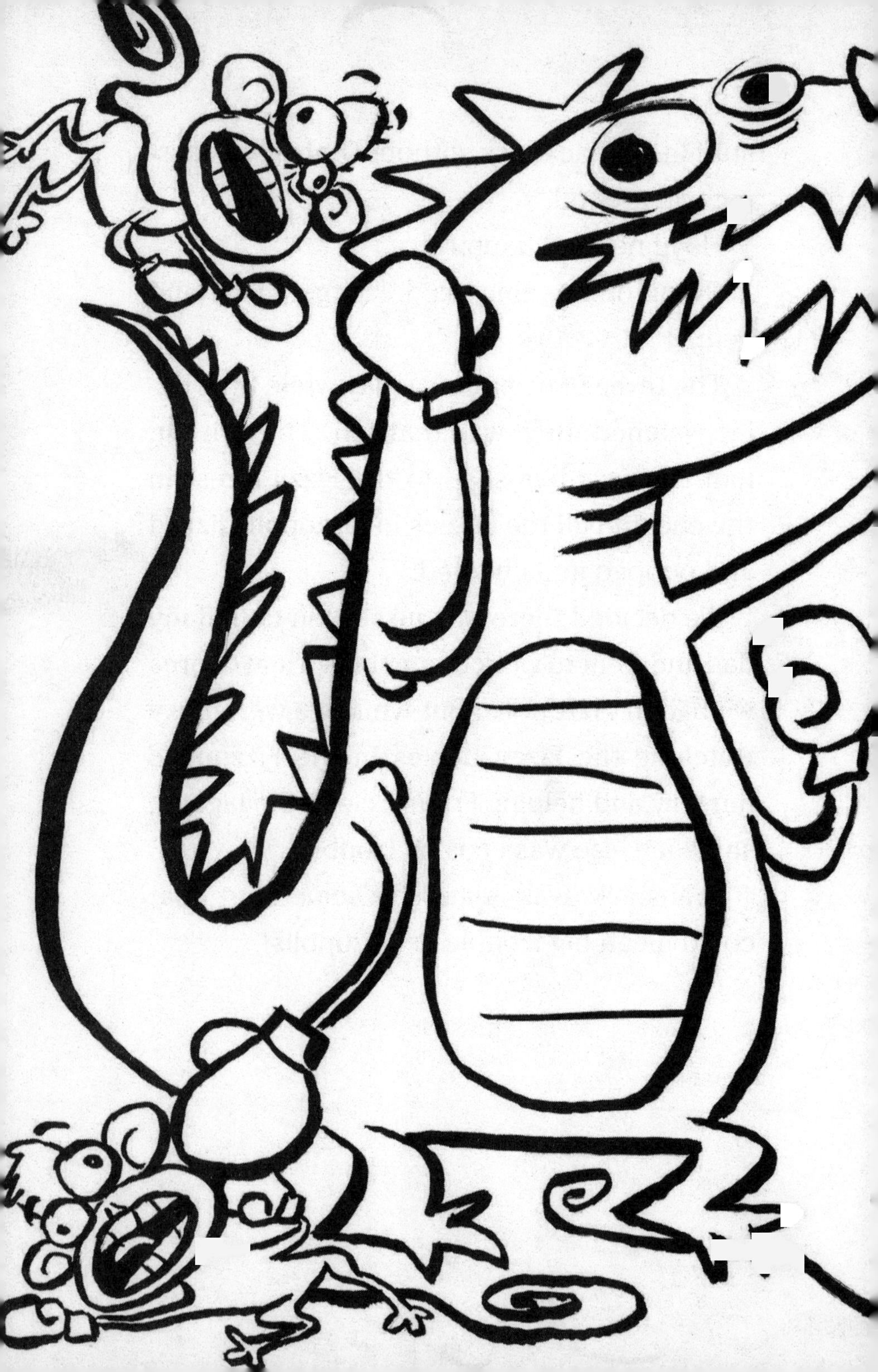

CHAPTER 4

The next morning was my favorite day of the week: Saturday. I could sleep in and when I got up there were old monster movies on television. They played them on the Pflugerville public access station, and Floyd loved watching giant lizards beat up big monkeys.

"Come on, my best good buddy. It's Saturday!" I said.

Floyd slept on a pillow next to me. When he heard the word "Saturday" he totally flipped out. He was all the way down the hallway and into the kitchen before I set one foot on the

floor. We always go to the kitchen first on Saturday mornings so we can make gigantic bowls of cereal.

"Hang on, Ima comin'!" I yelled. Then I did eleven cartwheels on my way to the kitchen. Floyd was already waiting with two bowls, the big kind we use to make cookie dough. I grabbed about ten cereal boxes and we poured a little bit from each one until both bowls were overflowing with graveyard mixes of awesome.

"Milk time!" I said, and I opened the refrigerator

door, where we usually kept a couple of gal-lons on hand.

I was just about to reach in and grab both gallons when I saw something unusual.

"Hey, look! It's my long-lost fart putty!"

Sitting right there on top of a block of ched-dar cheese was a glob of goopy green stuff. Floyd jumped onto my shoulder and peered into the fridge with me.

"That's super-duper strangomatic," he said.

"I know, right? What's my fart putty doing in the refrigerator?"

But Floyd didn't think it was my missing gag toy. Whatever it was made him nervous.

"What's wrong?"

Floyd mumbled some words I couldn't understand, and then he said, "Better show it to Dr. Fuzzwonker. I don't think that's fart putty."

I moved in closer and put my face right up next to the cheddar cheese block. It was cold in there. Upon closer inspection, I started to think maybe Floyd was right. Whatever that

gloppy green goop was, it didn't look exactly like my missing stuff.

I could feel a busy day coming on, so I suggested we eat a ton of cereal before finding my dad, and Floyd agreed. We were both hungry as bears, so we plowed through two gargantuan bowls of cereal in three minutes flat. After that I let Floyd brush my teeth and comb my hair (he enjoyed this routine more

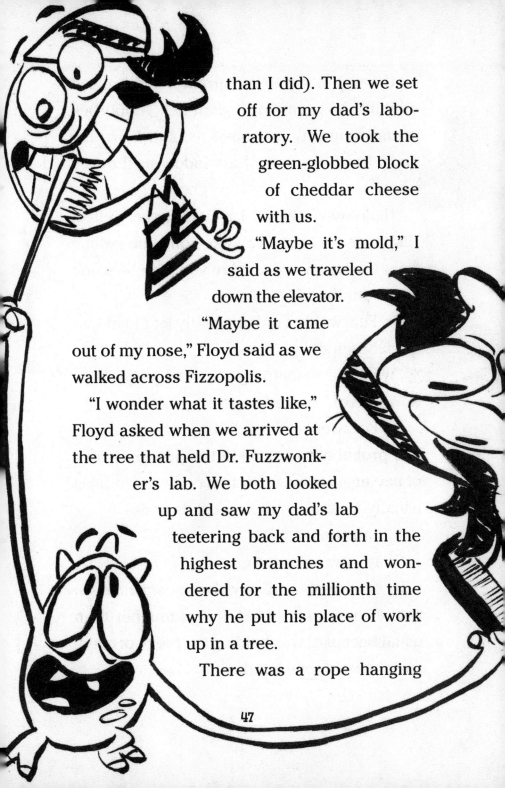

than I did). Then we set off for my dad's laboratory. We took the green-globbed block of cheddar cheese with us.

"Maybe it's mold," I said as we traveled down the elevator.

"Maybe it came out of my nose," Floyd said as we walked across Fizzopolis.

"I wonder what it tastes like," Floyd asked when we arrived at the tree that held Dr. Fuzzwonker's lab. We both looked up and saw my dad's lab teetering back and forth in the highest branches and wondered for the millionth time why he put his place of work up in a tree.

There was a rope hanging

47

all the way down to the ground, and I pulled on it like I was ringing a giant bell. A doorbell sound rang way up above us, and I saw my dad's head pop out of a window in the tree house.

"Hello down there!" Dr. Fuzzwonker yelled. His voice was far away like someone calling from across an ocean. "Are you sure he won't break anything?"

Dr. Fuzzwonker didn't usually let Floyd into the laboratory.

"We have something to show you. Come down here?" I asked.

Dr. Fuzzwonker's head disappeared into his lab, probably to calculate the pros and cons of having us come up or him come down. This usually took about nine seconds and—

"Climb aboard!"

Okay, seven seconds.

By "climb aboard" my dad meant hold on to the rope, which I did. It was tougher than usual because I was holding the block of cheddar cheese in one hand.

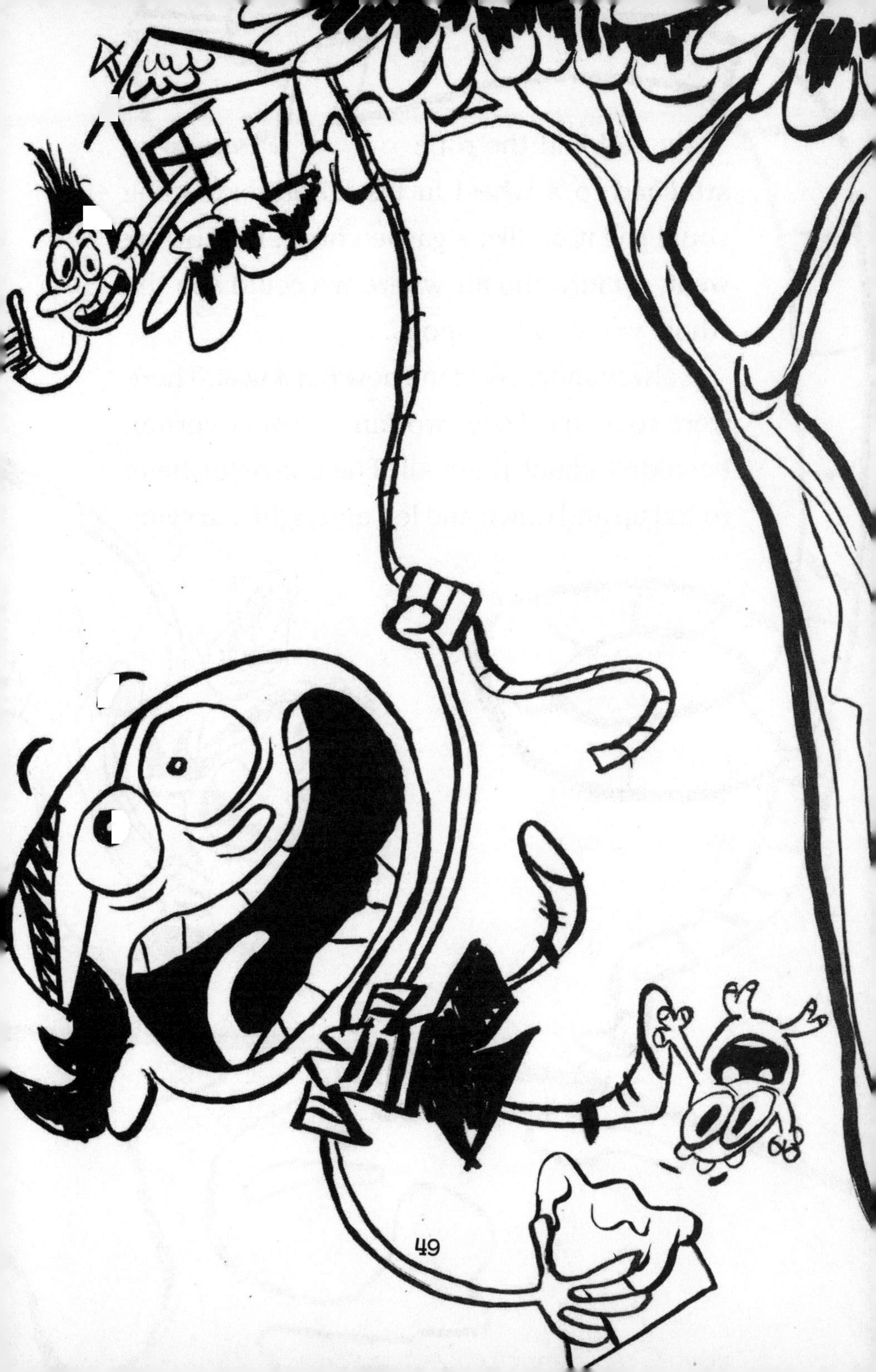

My dad had the rope
attached to a wheel in his laboratory so he
could roll it up like a garden hose. And off we
went, up into the air where we could see the
whole world of Fizzopolis.

It always surprised me how big it was. There
were so many Fizzies working in every corner,
I couldn't count them all. The conveyor belts
rolled up and down and left and right, carrying

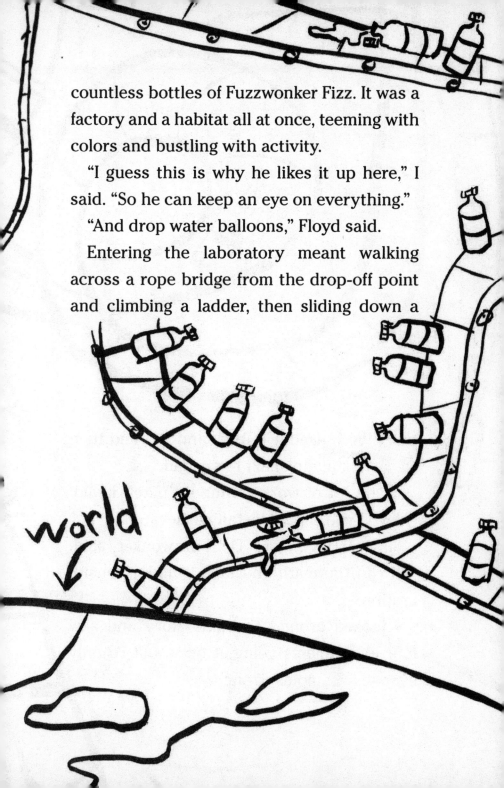

countless bottles of Fuzzwonker Fizz. It was a factory and a habitat all at once, teeming with colors and bustling with activity.

"I guess this is why he likes it up here," I said. "So he can keep an eye on everything."

"And drop water balloons," Floyd said.

Entering the laboratory meant walking across a rope bridge from the drop-off point and climbing a ladder, then sliding down a

world

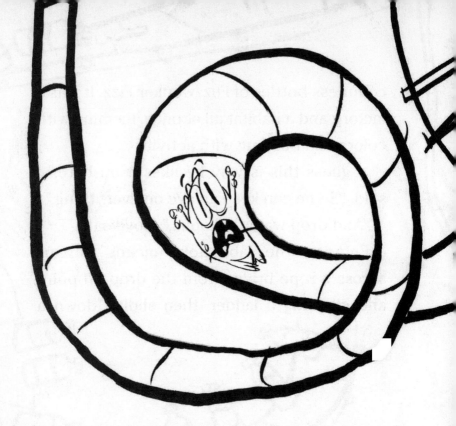

tube. We walked, climbed, and slid and then we were standing next to my dad.

"It's a lot of work getting up here," I said. "Maybe you should install an elevator."

"Interesting idea," Dr. Fuzzwonker said. "I'll run the math and take it under consideration."

I looked around the laboratory and saw four experiments going at once, but I'd only ever seen samples of one.

"Hey, the furry candy is getting more flavors," I said.

I shouldn't have said that because Floyd
loves sampling new fizzy candy. He dove off
my shoulder with an arc that looked like a
basketball heading into a hoop. Just before
Floyd landed, Dr. Fuzzwonker grabbed a but-
terfly net and held it over his experiment.
Floyd landed in the net and started flopping
around like a fish.

"We just ate a gallon of cereal," I said. "How can you be hungry?"

"If you don't mind, I'll put Floyd in the time-out tube while you're visiting," Dr. Fuzzwonker said.

"Good idea," I agreed, and Dr. Fuzzwonker turned the net over into a big glass container. Floyd bounced back and forth like a Ping-Pong ball until he tired himself out, and then he smashed his face up against the glass and watched us. He also fogged up the glass and started drawing messages with his finger like *I'm bored* and *I can't breathe* and *not fair!*

"We better make this fast," Dr. Fuzzwonker said. But I was so curious about the experiments that I waited to mention the block of cheddar cheese in my hand.

"Furry candy is looking good. Can I try one?" I asked.

Dr. Fuzzwonker took a pair of gorilla-sized tweezers out of his white lab coat and picked up an orange block about the size of a Lego. He held it right up next to my eyeball so I could get a good look at it. The fur was really thick, like shag carpet.

"Are you sure this thing is safe to ea—"

I didn't have time to finish asking whether or not I should put that thing in my mouth before Dr. Fuzzwonker jammed it in there. At first it felt like I had a hair ball on my tongue, but then it started to disintegrate

like cotton candy. There was some kind of far-out fizzy filling on the inside that tasted like oranges and chocolate mixed together.

"Wow, that was fantastic!" I laughed.

Dr. Fuzzwonker held up a mirror, and I saw that my teeth looked like they'd just gotten a serious spray tan.

"What the!" I said.

"It still needs some refining," Dr. Fuzzwonker said. "Be happy you didn't try the black one."

"How long are my teeth going to be orange?" I was thinking about not smiling all day at school on Monday.

I looked over at the time-out tube and Floyd had written a message in the fog on the glass. *Harold = dumb.*

"Don't worry," my dad said. "It will come off if you eat a banana."

My dad handed me a slice of banana on a toothpick and we moved to the next experiment. Over at the time-out tube, the fog read: *Floyd wants banana!*

"What's this one?" I asked as we came

across a bunch of beakers full of colorful balls.

"Exploding Jelly Beans," Dr. Fuzzwonker said. "But I wouldn't try one. They're harmless, but they have some problems."

My dad picked up a purple one and popped it in his mouth. It exploded and smoke started pouring out of his nose.

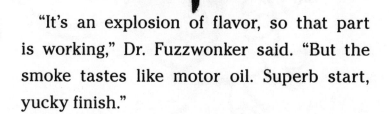

"It's an explosion of flavor, so that part is working," Dr. Fuzzwonker said. "But the smoke tastes like motor oil. Superb start, yucky finish."

We walked by another station that had something called Regenerating Ropes. They were licorice vines that grew back after you took a bite. "Very unstable," was all my dad said about those.

"I'll give one of these to Floyd," Dr. Fuzz-wonker said as he picked up something he called a Fabulayerous. It was chocolate on the outside, and it was the size of a baseball. He opened the hatch on the time-out tube and dropped it in, and we both watched Floyd go to work.

"There are seven hundred layers in a Fabu-layerous, all with different flavors. And there's ice cream in the middle."

"No way!" I said.

Floyd was through the first layer, but he had six hundred and ninety-nine to go.

That Fabulayerous was going to keep Floyd busy for quite a while, so it was the perfect time to tell my dad about the weird stuff we'd found in the refrigerator.

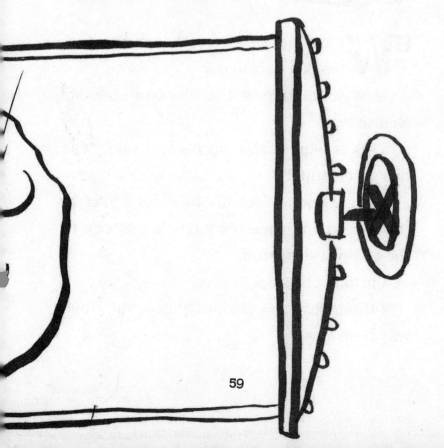

CHAPTER 5

"**W**hat's that you've got there?" Dr. Fuzz-wonker asked me.

He was pointing at the block of cheddar cheese.

"This is why I came up here," I said. "See this green stuff?"

Dr. Fuzzwonker put his face right next to the cheese and used his tongs to latch on to the gloppy green stuff.

"Curious," he said.

"I thought it was my fart putty, but Floyd wasn't so sure."

Dr. Fuzzwonker moved the specimen under a microscope and started dialing it in.

"Cheese!" he yelled.

"Really? That's weird."

"No, I mean I'm hungry. Slice me off some of that cheddar, will you?"

I used a butter knife I found lying next to the Fabulayerous samples and lopped off a piece of cheese. I handed it to my dad and he munched on it while he worked.

"Oh my," he said.

"What? What is it?" I asked.

"It's definitely not fart putty," he said. "It's something far more dangerous."

Fart putty is pretty dangerous stuff, so this was turning into a big deal. I looked over at Floyd, but he was busy making his way through layer number one hundred and twelve of that crazy Fabulayerous.

"Take a look," Dr. Fuzzwonker said. "But be warned: It's terribly disturbing."

I wasn't sure I wanted to see what gloppy green stuff looked like magnified a million times. Come to think of it, I didn't want to see what fart putty looked like magnified that much either. Who knows what kind of gross is in there. Curiosity won me over though, and I leaned next to the microscope.

"Dad, this is bizarro to the max."

My dad didn't respond and when I looked up he was cutting off another piece of cheese.

"It's . . . it's . . . ," I said. "It's moving!"

"I know," Dr. Fuzzwonker said as he ate more cheese. "Fascinating, don't you think?"

Whatever was under the microscope looked like the inside of a lava lamp.

"We better take a gander at the security footage," Dr. Fuzzwonker said.

"We have security footage?" I asked.

"Why, sure we do. Follow me."

There was a British soap opera playing in the corner of the lab on a television. I didn't notice until I got closer, but Grabstack was sitting in a miniature recliner watching the show. He was holding a thimble full of popcorn.

"I can't believe you let him come up here," I said. "What a blowhard."

"Can you believe I made the tiniest popcorn on earth?" Dr. Fuzzwonker said. "Too bad there's no market for it."

Dr. Fuzzwonker changed the channel to the security feeds and Grabstack threw a fit.

"Who has the gall to change the channel right when Romano is about to profess his

love to Margaret? This is research, people! Research!"

He looked up and saw me standing next to my dad. "What's *he* doing here?"

"I'm Dr. Fuzzwonker's kid. I can come up here whenever I want."

"Oh yeah?" Grabstack said. He got out of the recliner like he was going to punch me in the nose.

"You're kidding me," I said.

"Uh-oh," Dr. Fuzzwonker said.

Grabstack knew a troubling *uh-oh* when he heard one, and he turned back to the television. I caught a glimpse of Floyd before I looked at what Dr. Fuzzwonker had found on the security tapes, and Floyd's face was plastered against the glass of the time-out tube. His eyes were huge.

What the heck is everyone looking at? I wondered. When I turned to the television, I finally saw what everyone else did.

"Something has hijacked the Fizzomatic machine!" Dr. Fuzzwonker yelled.

Whatever it was, it was crawling out of the Fizzomatic machine like a giant stretchy piece of green cheese pizza.

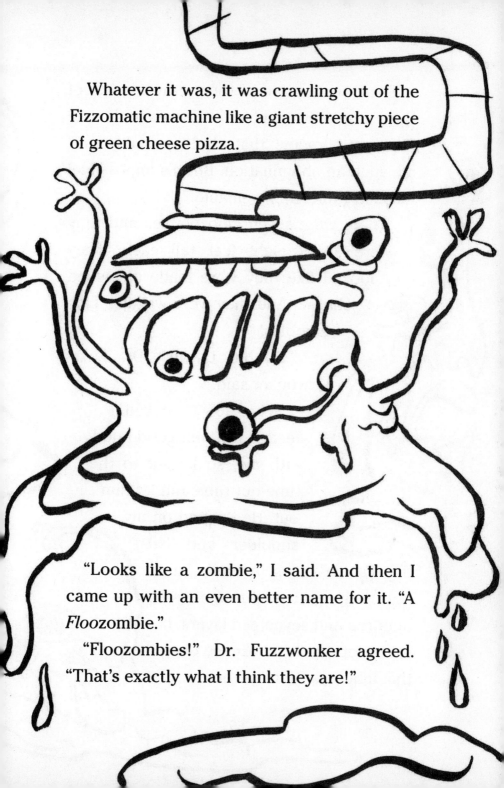

"Looks like a zombie," I said. And then I came up with an even better name for it. "A *Floo*zombie."

"Floozombies!" Dr. Fuzzwonker agreed. "That's exactly what I think they are!"

There were more of them crawling out of the Fizzomatic machine. "There's only one Fizzomatic recipe that could possibly create such an abomination. But it's impossible! Inconceivable! Unimaginable!"

There were seven Floozombies and they were about eight feet tall each. They looked like they were made of melted cheese. And they were walking. Like zombies!

"Double uh-oh," Dr. Fuzzwonker said.

"What now?" I asked. I needed my best good buddy with me, so I went to the time-out tube and let him out. He jumped on my shoulder and left the Fabulayerous behind. And he'd only gotten through two hundred and seventeen layers. It said a lot that he chose me over that fabulous Fabulayerous.

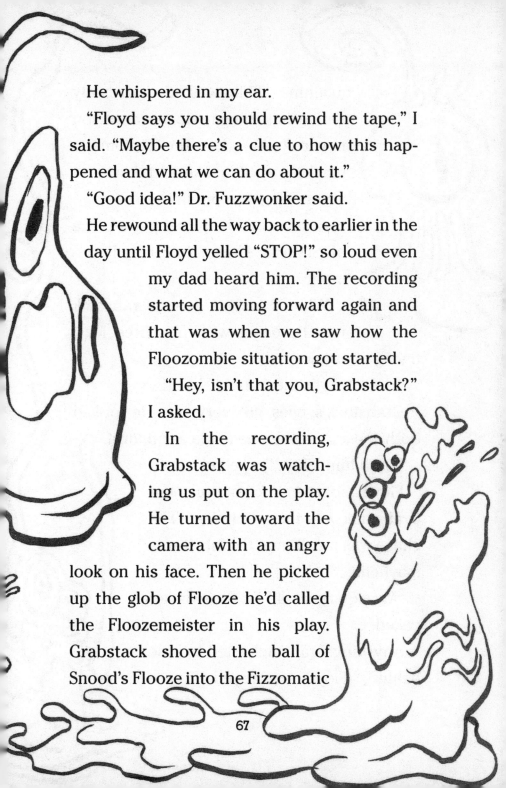

He whispered in my ear.

"Floyd says you should rewind the tape," I said. "Maybe there's a clue to how this happened and what we can do about it."

"Good idea!" Dr. Fuzzwonker said.

He rewound all the way back to earlier in the day until Floyd yelled "STOP!" so loud even my dad heard him. The recording started moving forward again and that was when we saw how the Floozombie situation got started.

"Hey, isn't that you, Grabstack?" I asked.

In the recording, Grabstack was watching us put on the play. He turned toward the camera with an angry look on his face. Then he picked up the glob of Flooze he'd called the Floozemeister in his play. Grabstack shoved the ball of Snood's Flooze into the Fizzomatic

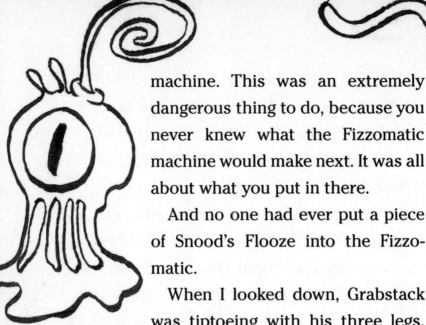

machine. This was an extremely dangerous thing to do, because you never knew what the Fizzomatic machine would make next. It was all about what you put in there.

And no one had ever put a piece of Snood's Flooze into the Fizzomatic.

When I looked down, Grabstack was tiptoeing with his three legs, trying to escape.

"Hold it right there, bub!" I said.

Grabstack's eyes got very big. He looked both ways. And then he made a run for it.

"Grab him, Floyd!" I yelled.

Floyd soared into action, but Grabstack was incredibly fast. The chase was on all over the lab. It was mayhem!

"My experiments!" Dr. Fuzzwonker yelled.

Anything Grabstack tried to hide behind, Floyd destroyed. There were beakers getting knocked over everywhere. One of them had about a hundred Exploding Jelly Beans in it and they flew into the air and exploded like firecrackers all over the lab. Floyd finally caught up to Grabstack and belly flopped on top of him.

"Good job, buddy!" I said. I slowly rolled Floyd off Grabstack and held that tiny little blowhard by the legs with two fingers.

"Let me go, you maniac!" Grabstack yelled, swinging his other leg at me.

"I knew I shouldn't have let Floyd up here," Dr. Fuzzwonker said as he shook his head.

I deposited Grabstack in the time-out tube and he stood on top of what was left of the Fabulayerous. Then he sat down and got sad on us. "I didn't know this would happen. How could I? I've made a terrible mistake."

There's nothing sadder than a two-inch-tall bummed-out British theater director.

"We know you didn't mean to do it," I said.

"We just need to focus on fixing the problem. We're dealing with a Floozombie outbreak. That sounds bad, but there's got to be a solution for it, right, Dad?"

Dr. Fuzzwonker scratched his nose. He scratched his ear. He scratched his head.

"This is a Fizzopolis-sized problem. I'm going to need time to find an antidote for these undead Floozombies. And clean up this laboratory."

Floyd was at the controls for the security footage, and we walked over to see what he'd found. He'd fast-forwarded to see where the

Floozombies had gone.

"Triple uh-oh," I said, because it finally occurred to me what a big problem this might be. I'd found the Floozombie sludge that looked like my fart putty upstairs in the refrigerator.

"They've escaped!" I screamed.

Looking at the security footage, we watched as all seven Floozombies walked into the elevator, the doors shutting behind them.

"They could be anywhere," Dr. Fuzzwonker said. "We'll have to divide and conquer."

"What does that mean?" Floyd said into my ear.

"Dad, you stay here and develop an antidote," I said. "Floyd and I will go searching for Floozombies in Pflugerville!"

It was up to me and Floyd to chase after them, and I knew exactly where we needed to go first.

"Come on, Floyd. We need to find Sammy."

It was going to take all three of us to track down an undead pack of Floozombies.

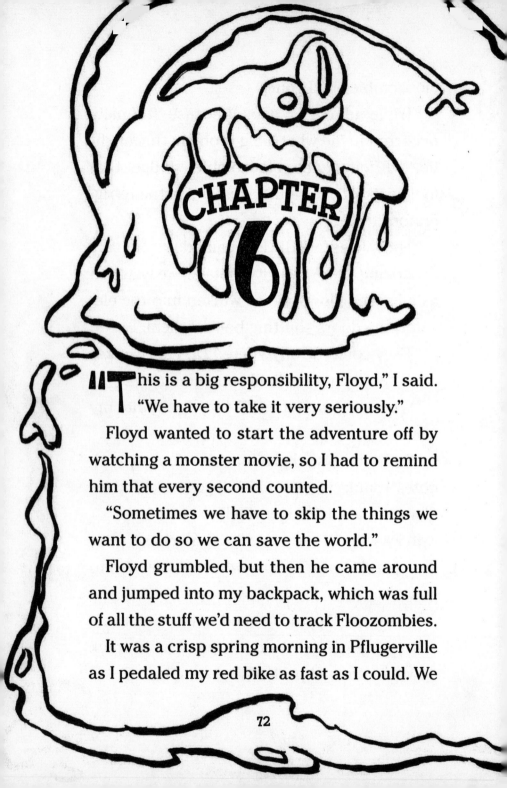

CHAPTER 6

"This is a big responsibility, Floyd," I said. "We have to take it very seriously."

Floyd wanted to start the adventure off by watching a monster movie, so I had to remind him that every second counted.

"Sometimes we have to skip the things we want to do so we can save the world."

Floyd grumbled, but then he came around and jumped into my backpack, which was full of all the stuff we'd need to track Floozombies.

It was a crisp spring morning in Pflugerville as I pedaled my red bike as fast as I could. We

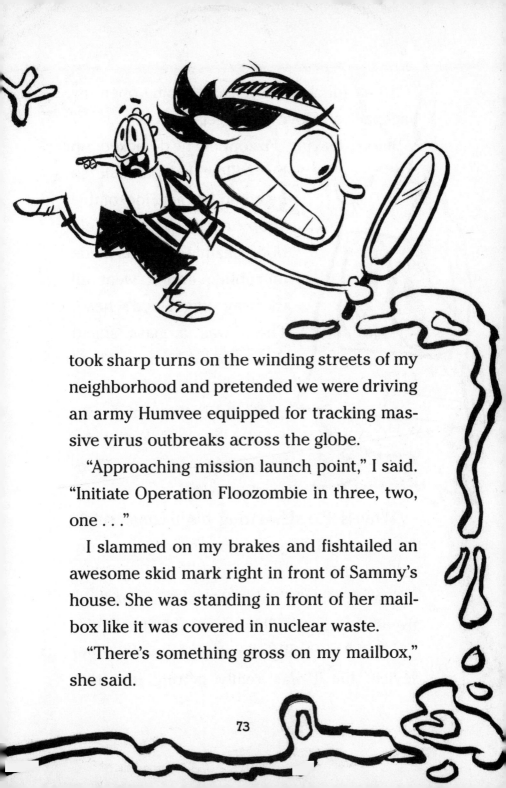

took sharp turns on the winding streets of my neighborhood and pretended we were driving an army Humvee equipped for tracking massive virus outbreaks across the globe.

"Approaching mission launch point," I said. "Initiate Operation Floozombie in three, two, one . . ."

I slammed on my brakes and fishtailed an awesome skid mark right in front of Sammy's house. She was standing in front of her mailbox like it was covered in nuclear waste.

"There's something gross on my mailbox," she said.

"Don't touch it!" I yelled, flipping open my backpack so Floyd could get out.

Before leaving Fizzopolis he'd picked up

his yellow hazmat suit so he could be our Floozombie goop collector. His full-body hazmat suit was made of rubber, and it went all the way over Floyd's head. There was a glass shield that covered his face. Floyd used the hazmat suit to clean the bathrooms in Fizzopolis. It was perfect for protecting him from Floozombie sludge.

"Why is Floyd wearing his hazmat suit?" Sammy asked. "Are you guys here to clean my bathrooms?"

"Stand back!" I said. "My sensor readings are off the charts. This area is infected."

I didn't actually have a sensor-reading device, but I was really getting into this

Operation Floozombie adventure.

"Removal tools," I said as I held my hand behind my head like I was searching for an arrow.

Floyd disappeared into the backpack and slapped a spatula into my hand. I put my other hand behind my head. "Containment unit."

Floyd dove into the backpack and milled around for a while, making all sorts of wacky noises. When he finally reappeared, Floyd set a Tupperware bowl in my hand.

"You guys are freaking me out," Sammy said.

"We've dealt with this before," I said, inching my way toward the mailbox as Floyd jumped on my shoulder. "Earlier today we had a cheddar cheese incident, and my dad said we should never, under any circumstances, touch Floozombie sludge. And we should be

prepared for it to try to attack us. Apparently exposure to the sun makes it more volatile."

"Huh?" Sammy said. She looked confused.

"There's no time to explain about the cheese event," I said. "Not until we contain this Floo-zombie sample."

"I'm going in," Floyd said. The hazmat helmet made him sound like he was on the moon relaying information back to NASA. Floyd jumped onto the pavement. When he started walking, his rubber suit made a squeaking noise every time he took a step. He thought this was hilarious, so he slowed down and sped up and did a couple of deep knee bends.

"Floyd!" I yelled. "This is no time to explore the amazing world of silly sounds. We've got serious work to do."

He mumbled something I couldn't make out and jumped up onto the top of the mailbox.

I moved in close and pried open the metal door with the spatula.

"Entering contamination zone," Floyd said. He grabbed the edge of the opening with both hands and flipped over into the mailbox.

I slammed the door shut.

"Are you sure that's a good idea?" Sammy asked.

"Better if we keep it locked up until we know what we're dealing with."

Floyd started banging into the sides so hard the pole holding up the mailbox began swaying back and forth.

"Sounds rough in there," Sammy said.

I started to worry that maybe Floyd was in trouble. "Maybe we should let him out."

Sammy opened the little door, and as soon as she did, a glob of Floozombie goop landed on her face. It knocked her backward and she landed on her butt.

"Floyd! It's on Sammy's face!" I said. "Red alert! Red alert!"

Floyd came flying out of the mailbox and

landed on top of the Floozombie sludge that was stuck to Sammy's face. He peeled up one edge and I got the spatula between Sammy's forehead and the green sludge.

"Pancake!" I said, and Floyd moved out of the way as I slid the spatula across Sammy's face and flipped the gob of green stuff like a short-order cook.

"Clear!" I screamed as the Floozombie sample rose into the air. Sammy and Floyd rolled in opposite directions, and I held the Tupperware in just the right spot. SPLAT! I caught the Floozombie sludge and covered it with the plastic lid all in one fluid move.

"Contamination contained," I proclaimed proudly. "Begin cleanup."

Dr. Fuzzwonker had done just enough testing from the cheese incident to create a Floozombie cleaning solution.

"Don't move," I told Sammy. "This Floozombie spray will fix you right up."

My dad had put the Floozombie cleaning solution into a nose-spray bottle. I shot Sammy in the face with it.

"Hey! You got some in my eye!"

"It's okay," I said, and then I sprayed her again. "Better to make sure it's all cleaned up. According to my dad, an untreated Floozombie encounter could lead to Floozombie-like behavior."

"Wait, what?" Sammy said as she wiped her face off. "So I could turn into a zombie?"

"More like a cheese zombie," I said. "But you're fine. This area is one hundred percent cleaned."

Sammy patted me on the shoulder. "You guys are the weirdest friends ever. Also, thank you for saving my face."

"You're welcome." I nodded and smiled.

Floyd landed back on my shoulder and talked into my ear.

"Floyd thinks we could use some help tracking down these strange creatures. I was thinking the same thing."

"I have no idea what you're talking about, but I'd love to," Sammy said. "I'll get the Green Pickle!"

The Green Pickle is Sammy's bike. It has a banana seat and a sissy bar and it's mostly green.

Floyd stored the Floozombie sample in the backpack and stayed out of sight while we continued through the neighborhood. I figured if the Floozombies left my house and walked to Sammy's, they probably kept going in the same direction. All we needed to do was follow the trail through Pflugerville.

The hunt was officially on.

CHAPTER
7

While we rode, I filled Sammy in on everything that was going on.

"Grabstack is such a dweeb," Sammy said. "I can't believe he created a Floozombie invasion."

We rode by the Pflugerville bowling alley and a family of four ran out the door screaming, got into their station wagon, and drove away.

"Looks like trouble," I said. "We better get in there."

Inside we found what we were looking for

on lane number five. People were standing around in a circle, including Mo, the guy who owned the place. It was called Mo's Bowl-A-Rama.

"Coming through," Sammy said. "Step aside, folks—we may be dealing with a virus outbreak."

That cleared the place in a hurry. Everyone but Mo ran for the exits. Dr. Fuzzwonker was the most famous scientist in Pflugerville, so Mo knew if Harold and his friends were talking virus outbreak, he had to take it seriously.

"This is terrible for business!" Mo said. Mo was a short, round guy with a bald head and a bubble nose. Everything about him screamed bowling ball. "I'm calling the PPCD!"

The PPCD was the Pflugerville Pest Control Department, and we definitely wanted to be gone by the time they got to Mo's Bowl-A-Rama. While Mo went to call the PPCD, Floyd sprang into action. And by action, I don't mean searching for Floozombie samples. He picked up the first bowling ball he saw and lifted it over his head. The ball was bigger than he was by a long shot, but Floyd is a strong little dude so he had no problem running down the lane in his squeaky rubber pants and throwing it over his head. Just before he threw the ball I realized what a big mistake it was: A glob of Floozombie sludge was stuck on the ball like a wad of gum.

"Don't throw that ball!" I yelled, but it was too late. Luckily, Floyd had no idea how to bowl, so he threw the ball straight up in the air. It landed with a giant BANG on the wood floor right in front of us and rolled into the gutter.

"He's good," Sammy said.

"Let's get to work, team," I said.

The impact of being slammed into the floor must have made the Floozombie glob nervous, because it was moving fast along the curved surface of the bowling ball. Before we

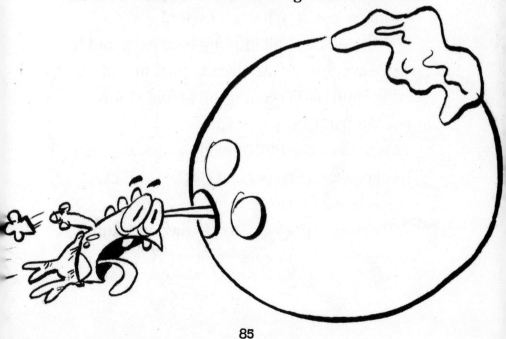

could use the spatula treatment, it slid right down into one of the finger holes.

"Maybe we should just take the whole thing," Sammy advised. "I don't think it's going to come out of that hole."

It was the fastest way to get out of here and keep searching, so I taped the hole shut with a strip of silver duct tape. Then I took the ball up to Mo.

"I'm going to need to quarantine this bowling ball," I said. "I'll bring it back when I finish."

"Be my guest," Mo said. "There's no one bowling anyway. What a disaster."

I dropped the ball into my backpack and it was heavy. But it was already past lunchtime and we still hadn't found the actual Floozombies. We had to keep moving.

We passed the PPCD team on the way out. They were wearing normal clothes and carrying leashes and cages.

"They don't even have hazmat suits," Sammy said. "Amateurs."

Our journey led us farther afield, past Pflugerville Elementary School and into the miniature golf course. We did an extraction there that took almost an hour on hole number twelve. The Floozombie sludge was hiding in the windmill feature where Floyd could go to work without being seen. "These Floozombies were really busy last night," Sammy said.

"We're almost to the edge of Pflugerville," Sammy said when we kept going. "I hope they didn't wander all the way out of town."

We passed the Pflugerville supermarket but didn't find any sign of trouble there.

We visited a gas station, a Laundromat, a car wash, and the Pflugerville Hamburger Shack—all those places came up clean.

"It's getting late," I said as I watched the sun touch down on the trees. "Another hour and it will be dark."

"Floozombies and nighttime," Sammy said. "That feels like a bad combo."

We pulled into the only used car lot in town and did some wheelies in the parking lot.

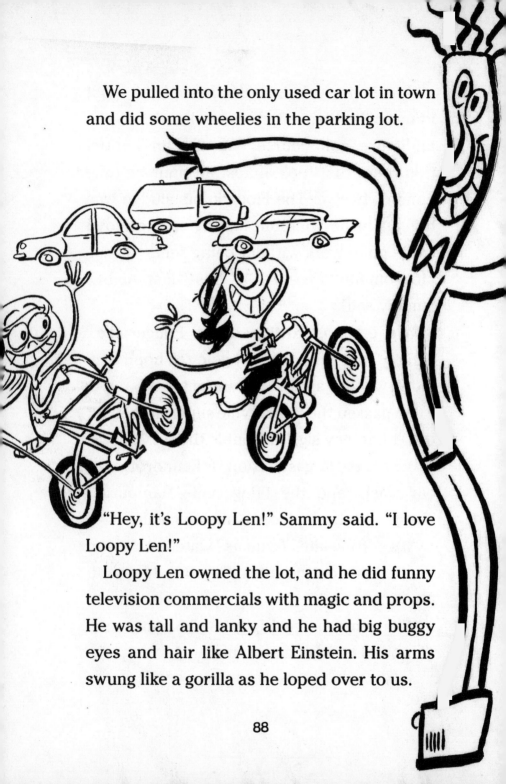

"Hey, it's Loopy Len!" Sammy said. "I love Loopy Len!"

Loopy Len owned the lot, and he did funny television commercials with magic and props. He was tall and lanky and he had big buggy eyes and hair like Albert Einstein. His arms swung like a gorilla as he loped over to us.

"Hello, Harold Fuzzwonker. How's your dad doing these days?" he asked.

Loopy Len and Dr. Fuzzwonker were in the same bridge club.

"He's in the middle of a very important research project," I said as I pointed to Sammy. "This is my super-duper palamino, Sammy. She's a fan of your loopy commercials."

"I think you're hilarious," Sammy said.

Loopy Len pulled a rubber chicken out of his back pocket and started having a conversation with it.

"Listen, Len," I said. I didn't have time for him to go into a whole comedy routine. "Have you seen anything odd today? Dr. Fuzzwonker sent us out looking for . . . for . . ."

"Let me guess," Loopy Len said. "It's top secret."

"Yes!" I agreed.

"It usually is with your dad," Len said as he put the rubber chicken back in his pocket. He put a fake nose and glasses on and Sammy snorted with laughter. "When I left last night there was a 1956 AMC Rambler parked right there. Now it's gone."

Len was staring at an empty spot on the lot.

"And I found this gloppy stuff on the pavement."

Loopy Len held up a small glass jar. It was filled with Floozombie sludge.

"This is very interesting information, Len," I said. "Would you mind if we took that sample with us so my dad can do some experiments on it?"

"Be my guest," Len said. He handed me

the little jar and put a fake arrow through his head. "You two are old enough to drive, aren't you? I'll make you a heck of a deal on that car if you can locate it."

"I'm only ten," Sammy said. "But we'll try to find your missing car all the same."

Sammy had Loopy Len sign her arm before we left and he reminded us to watch his new car ads that would start airing on Pflugerville public television.

"I'll be wearing a pink bunny suit," he said.

"Classic." Sammy beamed.

As we rode away the day started turning to night and Floyd crawled out onto my shoulder. He had taken the hazmat helmet off.

"It was getting stuffy in there," he said. "And

crowded in that bag. I keep ending up under the bowling ball."

"Sorry, little buddy," I said. "If we weren't in such a rush I'd take that darn bowling ball to Dr. Fuzzwonker right now."

"Harold," Sammy said. "It's officially dark outside."

"Turn on your bike headlight," I said. "We have to keep searching. Who knows how much trouble these Floozombies will cause if they roam around all night."

Off in the distance we could see the Snood Candy Factory at the very edge of town. The towering smokestack was billowing candy-flavored steam. And that's when it hit me. How could I have been so mind-numbingly dense?

"Of course! The Floozombies were created when Grabstack threw Snood's Flooze into the Fizzomatic machine!"

Sammy started nodding and we both pedaled faster. "So there's only one thing they want to eat. Snood's Flooze!"

"They must have followed the smell from

the smokestack for miles and miles," I said.

If we were going to find the missing Floo-zombies, we'd find them at the Snood Candy Factory.

CHAPTER 8

It was dark as we made our way down the private Snood driveway. It was even darker inside the covered bridge, which is probably why we almost ran right into a 1956 AMC Rambler. When we came to the bridge we were hauling donuts (this means going really, really fast). It was a good thing we had our headlights on or we'd have slammed right into the Rambler. Instead, Sammy and I hit the brakes and stopped just short of the trunk.

"Rambler," Sammy said. "Looks like we found Loopy Len's missing car."

"And all the doors are open," I added as I dropped my bike and walked around the driver's side. The bowling ball in my backpack made it feel like I was carrying the anchor for an aircraft carrier.

"There's a ton of Floozombie gunk over here," Sammy said as she went around the other side of the car.

"Same thing on this side," I said. "Those Floozombies totally stole this car."

We got back on our bikes and hightailed it for the Snood Candy Factory.

Floyd got right up in my ear and started yammering.

"What did he say?" asked Sammy.

"He wants some Snood's Flooze," I said. "As much as we can carry." I could hardly blame him, since it was already an hour past dinnertime.

Floyd made a lot of *yum yum* sounds as the Snood Candy Factory came into view. It loomed dark and scary against the night sky, and I wondered if maybe we were in over our heads.

"Let's get a little closer and see if we can hear anything," Sammy said. She got off the Green Pickle and started walking without her headlight.

I felt Floyd move off my shoulder and return to the backpack and figured he was too scared to watch whatever happened next. But I couldn't let Sammy go it alone, so I got off my bike and caught up to her.

"Hey! What are you nitwits doing here?"

We both knew the annoying voice coming from behind us. It was Garvin Snood.

"And who parked their car on our private driveway? I barely got my bike past that old junker."

"Oh, hey, Garvin," I said. "How are you? We're fine. We're just hanging around is all. Nothing happening here. Just a lot of standing around."

"Yeah, right," Garvin said. He was wearing his football uniform, which was way too big for him. The shoulder pads stuck out so far it made his head look like the size of an orange. He must have been coming home from Pee Wee football practice.

"Stay right where you are," Garvin sneered. "I'm getting my dad."

Garvin took off for the main door of the candy factory and we yelled for him to stop. He wouldn't listen though, so we ran after him. I'm fast, but Sammy is even faster. She's like lightning. Plus, I was carrying a bowling ball on my back. Anyway, Sammy caught up to Garvin and tackled him like a pro bowl linebacker. Garvin did a belly flop right into the dirt.

"Don't go in there, Garvin!" I shouted, but Garvin Snood was very bullheaded. If he wanted to go into the Snood Candy Factory, then he was going to do it. He bolted upright

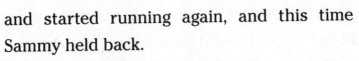

and started running again, and this time Sammy held back.

"He's not going to listen," she said. "What are we going to do?"

Garvin reached the gigantic wooden door of the factory and pulled out his special key to get inside. When he had the door open, he looked back at us and laughed.

"Get ready for trouble, losers!"

Garvin kept on laughing, but then an arm that looked like melted green cheese reached through the opening and pulled him inside.

"This is crazy!" I yelled. Floyd came out of the backpack and stood on my shoulder while we crept closer to the door. It was still open a little bit so we could peek inside.

"Let's take a quick look and see what we're dealing with," Sammy said.

We got right up next to the opening and we couldn't see anything, so we opened the door a little bit more. It made a terrible squeak, but at least we could all see inside the factory. Floyd jumped off my shoulder and stood by my feet.

"Looks like we found what we were looking for," Sammy said.

"No kidding," I agreed.

The Floozombies were definitely in there. They'd completely taken over the place. Tanks full of Flooze had been tipped over, and Mr. Snood was stuck to one of the walls.

It looked like he'd been thrown against a thousand bottles of Elmer's glue and all he could do was flail around like an insect stuck in honey. Garvin wasn't faring much better. He was running around the factory screaming his head off. It looked like he might have peed his pants, but it was hard to tell through all that football equipment.

But then one of the Floozombies started coming toward us. His globby arms were reaching in our direction and he was getting way too close, way too fast. This was getting totally bonkers in a hurry!

I should have slammed the door shut, but instead I was distracted by a noise I knew all too well from the ground by my feet. Floyd was standing there with a bottle of Fuzzwonker Fizz. The sound I'd heard was him popping the top and starting to guzzle it in big whopping gulps. "NoOOOooOOOoooOOOoOOOoOoooOoO!" I screamed.

Floyd was acting like he was watching one of our favorite monster movies back at the house.

"Give me that bottle, you nitwit!" I said. Sammy and I both tried to grab the bottle, but I got there first and pulled as hard as I could. Floyd had already downed half of it, so once I got it free from his mouth he let loose a huge burp right in my face.

It was an A+ effort, but the bottle flew out of both our hands and through the door. We looked up and watched it flip end over end and bonk the Floozombie right in its cheesy

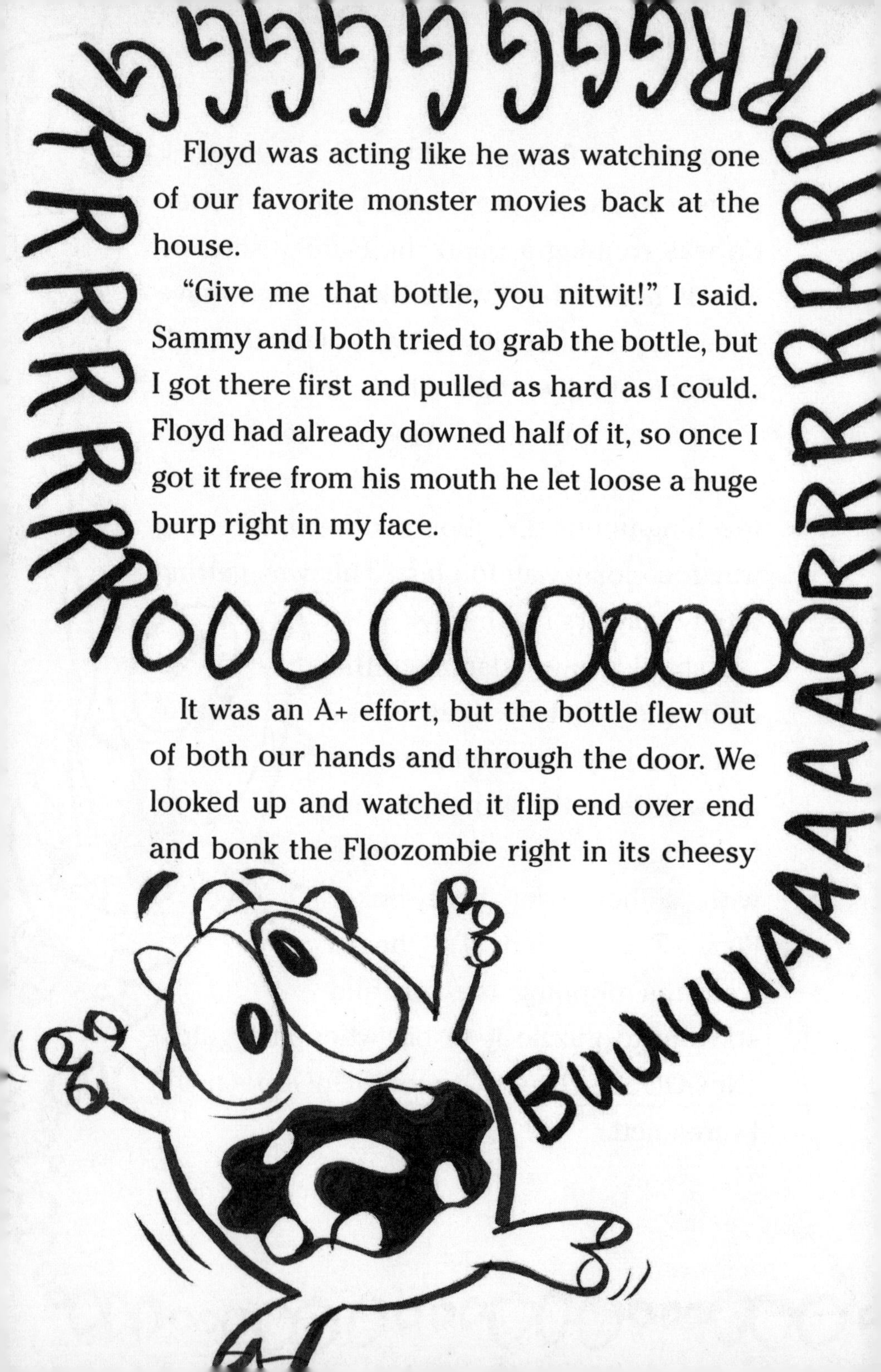
BUUUAAARRRRRRRRGGGGGGGGGGGRRRRRRRRROOOOOOOOOOO

green head. The Fuzzwonker Fizz fell to the floor of the factory and poured out in fizzy pops and fizzles.

"You guys," Sammy said. "Look!"

I couldn't believe my eyes.

UUUBLLAAAAAA

All this time the antidote for Floozombies was right in front of us. Of course! Floozombie Kryptonite had to be Fuzzwonker Fizz. It was too perfect.

"He's melting," Sammy said.

The Floozombie stepped right into the puddle of fizz and looked down as smoke started rising into the air. One of his cheesy toes melted into the pool, but then he kept walking.

"He's still coming this way—with only nine toes!" I said. "Run!"

I slammed the door shut and locked it with the key Garvin Snood left behind. Then I kneeled down and picked up my best good buddy.

"Floyd, you're a genius," I said.

"Why, thank you," he replied. "And you owe me one half bottle of Fuzzwonker Fizz."

I ran to my bike and wished for the tenth time that day that I was not carrying a bowling ball on my back.

"Come on, you guys," I said. "I know exactly what we need to do."

I had an idea. A BIG idea. But we'd have to move fast before the Floozombies destroyed the Snood Candy Factory and more than likely exposed the biggest secret in the world in the process. Fizzopolis!

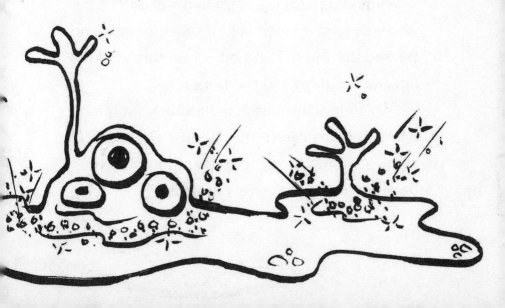

CHAPTER 9

"**W**here are we going?" Sammy asked as our headlights cut through the darkness.

"Back to Fizzopolis," I said. "I've got a plan, but we need to make a few stops along the way."

When we passed Loopy Len's used car lot, we zigzagged between all the cars for sale and parked in front of Len's office. He was working late, and Sammy did the honors.

"We found the missing Rambler," she said when he answered the door. "There's still some cleanup work, but we should have it back to you by tomorrow morning."

"That's excellent news!" Loopy Len said. He squirted water in Sammy's face with a gag pen, and then handed it to her and told her she could keep it. "Use it wisely. Not everyone likes that joke."

"Will do, sir," Sammy said. "And thanks!"

We got back on our bikes and rode like maniacs until we reached the bowling alley. I had Sammy ride ahead and open the door.

"I've removed all the Floozombie sludge," Floyd told me as he handed me the bowling ball. "It's safe for knocking down pins again."

"Good job, buddy," I said. "Let's test it out."

I rode right through the open door and past the arcade machines. When I passed Mo at the front desk, I yelled, "Bowling ball is all fixed up. She's ready to roll."

I rode my bike down two steps onto lane number three and bowled that ball for a strike. But my bike got caught in the gutter and I had to do some fast thinking to bunny hop into the next lane and hightail it for home.

#3

"Nice throw," Sammy said when I rode out the door into the night.

"Thanks," I said. "I'm glad I don't have to carry that thing around anymore."

"Me, too," Floyd said. He was back on my shoulder. "It was getting really crowded in there."

Another ten minutes and we were back at the house, down the elevator, and standing

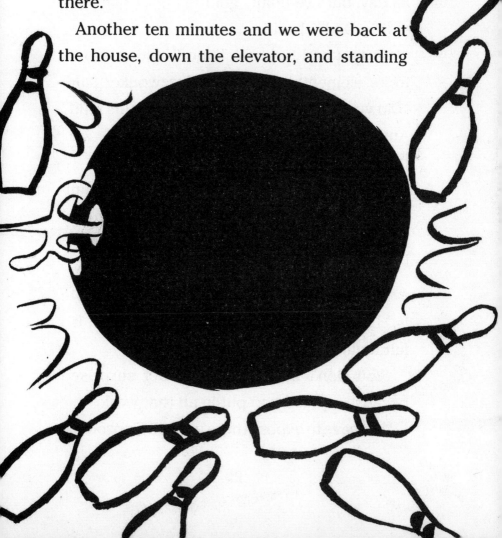

in my dad's laboratory. Grabstack was still in the time-out tube, glumly licking the Fabulay-erous. I felt bad for him, but there was no time for dealing with that now.

"I've figured out the antidote!" Dr. Fuzz-wonker yelled at the top of his lungs. "It took all day, but I've finally got it!"

"Uh, Dad?" I said.

"First, I had to break Snood's Flooze down to its elemental parts," Dr. Fuzzwonker said. "Did you know there was broccoli in this stuff? And radishes. Also, a lot of sugar."

"Dad, listen—" I said.

"Then I had to reorganize all the ingredi-ents in rank order, add two parts condensed milk, and liquefy them with a blender."

"And what you figured out was—" I said.

"And you'll never believe what the antidote is," Dr. Fuzzwonker said. "It's astounding! It's miraculous! It's Fuzzwonker Fizz!"

"You don't say?" I tried to act surprised because my dad had put in all that work.

"We have to expose these undead Floozombie

thingamabobs to a large amount of Fuzzwonker Fizz, and it will turn them back into plain old Snood's Flooze."

"Wait a second here," Sammy said. "How much Fuzzwonker Fizz are we talking about?"

Dr. Fuzzwonker did a whole bunch of calculations on his computer.

"Two hundred gallons of Fuzzwonker Fizz per Floozombie should do it."

"Two hundred gallons!" Sammy screamed. "That means we need one thousand four hundred gallons of Fuzzwonker Fizz."

"That's a lot of Fizz," Floyd said in my ear.

"I was afraid of that," I added. But I had already thought of this. Seeing the damage half a bottle of Fuzzwonker Fizz had done back at the Snood Candy Factory had gotten me thinking. "I know exactly what we need to do. Follow me, everyone."

I stopped short when I arrived at the time-out tube. Poor little Grabstack had the saddest look on his face. His tiny chin was bobbing up and down like he was about to cry.

"You know," I said to Floyd. "We don't have school at night. Maybe you could take a travel buddy along with us. But only if you want."

Floyd mumbled like he was trying to decide, then he talked into my ear. "Can I bring the Fabulay-erous, too?"

"You can," I said.

Floyd jumped onto the table where the time-out tube was, and I took the lid off so he could get inside. He and Grabstack had a conversation I couldn't hear and then they hugged.

"Awwww. They're too cute," Sammy said.

"Come on, you guys," I said. "We need to move fast."

I put Grabstack, Floyd, and the Fabulay-erous into my backpack and started for the rope.

"Dad, you stay here and rev up the

Fizzomatic machine—I need one thousand four hundred gallons pronto!"

"I'm on it!" Dr. Fuzzwonker said. He went immediately to work on a lot of dials and levers that I didn't understand and lowered us to the ground using one of his feet for the rope controls.

"Your dad is very talented," Sammy said. "But that's a lot of Fuzzwonker Fizz. And how are we ever going to carry that much?"

"I have that figured out," I said as we raced through Fizzopolis and arrived at the lagoon.

"Hey, Franny!" I yelled into the swampy water. "I need a favor."

Franny was already full of swamp water, and she blew it out with a loud honking noise. Her job was to keep the lagoon clean, and she did that by sucking in yucky water and blowing out clean water. It was her special talent.

She arrived next to us and made some honking and wheezing noises.

"Franny, do you think you could hold one thousand four hundred gallons of Fuzzwonker Fizz?"

Franny's eyes got about as big as dinner plates. She started shaking like a scared Chihuahua.

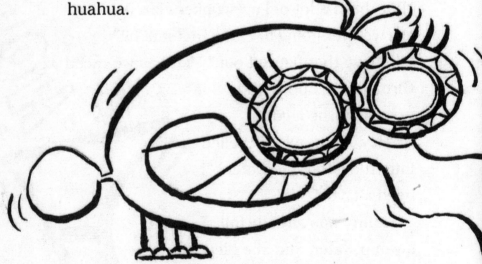

"It's super important," I added. "Fizzopolis is depending on you!"

Franny got a determined look on her face and rubbed her belly.

"Froobaglaglablaglablagob," Franny said.

"Floyd," I said. "Translation, please."

Grabstack's head popped out of my backpack. "We're in rehearsals, you buffoon! My actors need their space. And Franny says she can do it."

"Excellent!" Sammy said. "Thanks, Grabstack. How's the play coming along?"

"It's riddled with problems. We'll never make the premiere!"

"Better get back to it then," I said, mostly because I wanted to get rid of him as fast as I could.

"Come on, Franny. Let's get this show on the road."

And then I put part two of my plan to rid the world of Floozombies into play.

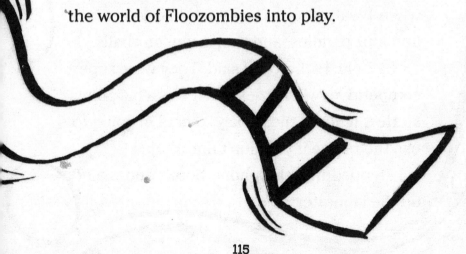

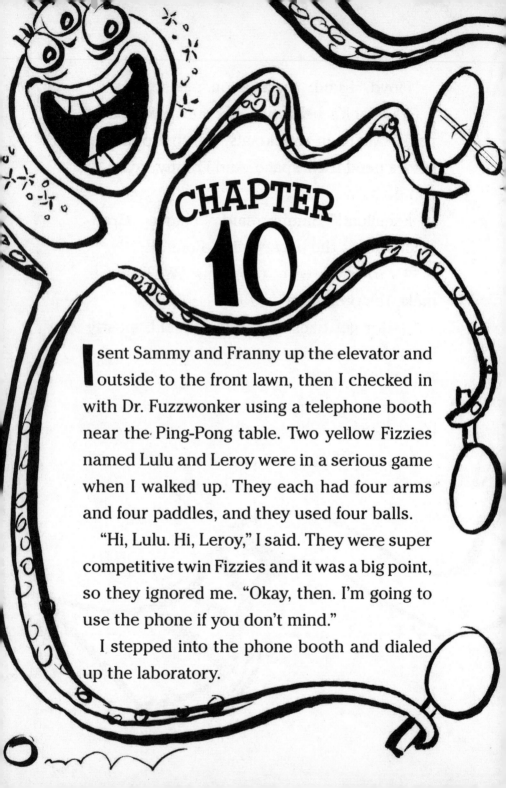

CHAPTER 10

I sent Sammy and Franny up the elevator and outside to the front lawn, then I checked in with Dr. Fuzzwonker using a telephone booth near the Ping-Pong table. Two yellow Fizzies named Lulu and Leroy were in a serious game when I walked up. They each had four arms and four paddles, and they used four balls.

"Hi, Lulu. Hi, Leroy," I said. They were super competitive twin Fizzies and it was a big point, so they ignored me. "Okay, then. I'm going to use the phone if you don't mind."

I stepped into the phone booth and dialed up the laboratory.

"How's it going up there?" I asked. I could see the Fizzomatic machine about fifty yards away and, man, it was really chugging.

"I'm up to one thousand gallons, but it's pushing everything we've got!" Dr. Fuzz-wonker said. "You'll need to start pumping so I can backfill. We've reached capacity!"

I ran to the Fizzomatic machine and found about a dozen Fizzy creatures working fever-ishly to keep my dad's contraption from blowing up. Some of them were replacing riv-ets as they exploded off the hull. Other Fizzies

were using duct tape to patch up seams where the metal had expanded from so much Fuzzwonker Fizz. Another Fizzy was using a blowtorch to weld a part back on that had fallen off. It was chaos!

The Fizzomatic machine was equipped with a very long hose for distributing Fuzzwonker Fizz to different places inside Fizzopolis. It was rolled up on a giant wheel, and two more blue Fizzies were standing there waiting for me.

"We better hurry!" I said. "You guys unroll, I'll run to the elevator."

I grabbed the hose and started running while the blue Fizzies rolled more and more hose out. I'd already determined that Franny full of one thousand four hundred gallons of Fuzz-wonker Fizz was not going to fit in the elevator. We were going to have to fill her up on the street in front of my house. Good thing it was dark out there or we'd never keep Fizzopolis a secret.

The hose was getting really heavy and I slowed down. Then I came to a complete stop. I looked back and saw the Fiz-zomatic machine expanding and leaking and smoking. The Fizzies were doing everything they could, but we were running out of time.

"Floyd!" I yelled as loud as I could. "I need help!"

Floyd was on my shoulder in a flash. I knew the play was important to him, but when I really needed help, I could always count on my best good buddy.

Floyd jumped on top of my head and put his paws in his mouth. Then he let out the loudest whistle I'd ever heard. Fizzies came running from every corner of Fizzopolis. Small ones, round ones, tall ones, skinny ones— there were more Fizzies than I could count, and they all grabbed a section of hose behind me and started heaving us forward.

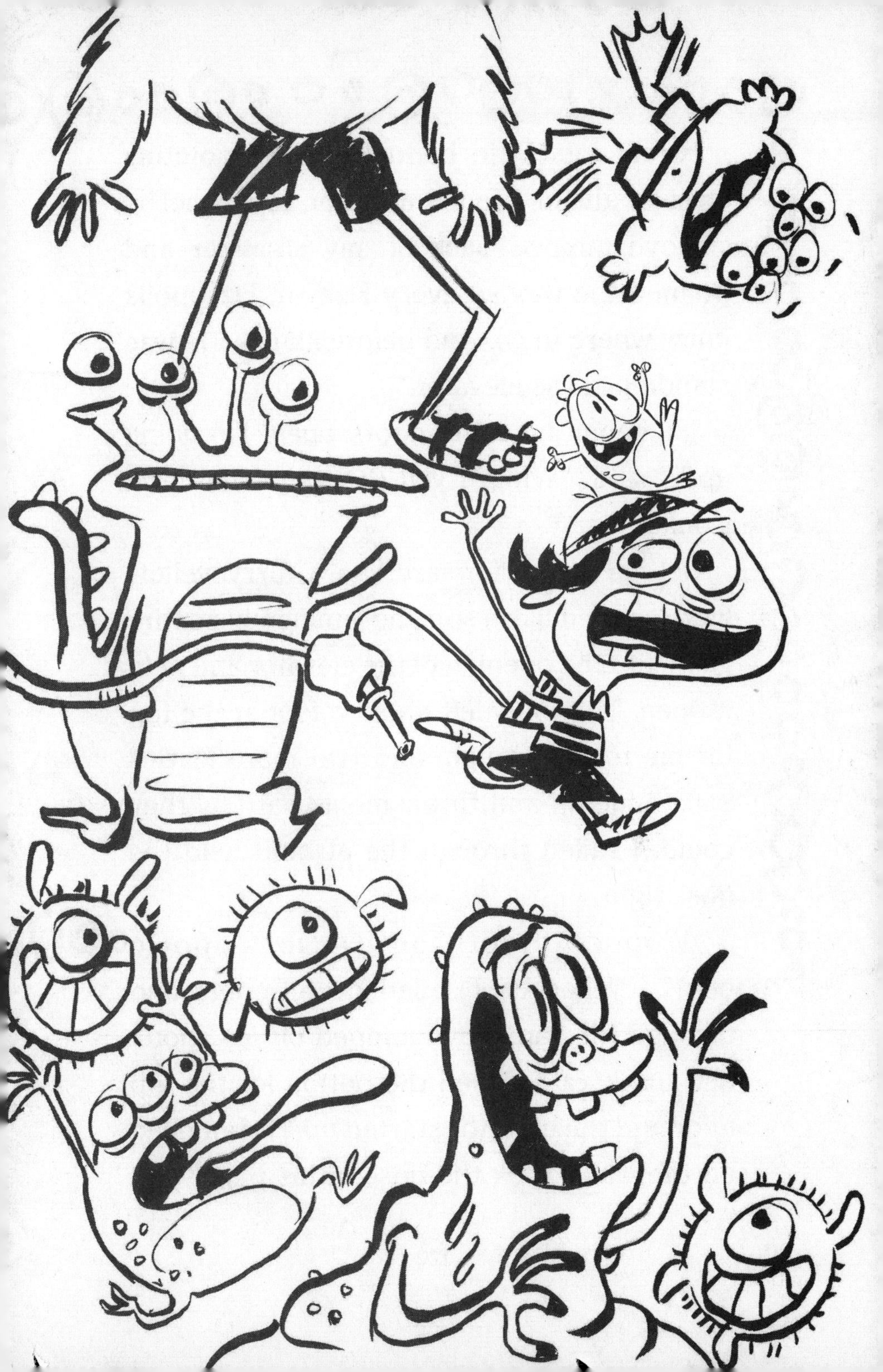

"Great job, little buddy!" I said, pointing straight ahead. "To the elevator, everyone!"

Floyd jumped back on my shoulder and pointed the way so every Fizzy in Fizzopolis knew where to go. And before I knew it, I was standing in the elevator.

"Someone hold the doors open. I'm going up," I said. "When I yell GO, send the Fuzz-wonker Fizz!"

George rolled forward. As a furry yellow Fizzy shaped like a sofa, he jammed his entire girth into the opening of the elevator and held it open. That only left about a foot at the top for me to fit through, and two more Fizzies picked me up and threw me as hard as they could. I sailed through the air and held the hose tight.

"WoooooooHooOOooOOoOoOoooooOooOoo!" I yelled as I sailed over George and through the gap. Floyd jumped off my shoulder and karate kicked the button for the top floor and the elevator started up. He bounced off the walls, took the hose in his paws, and tied it to the elevator rail in a grand total of four seconds.

"Floyd, you are amazing," I said as the elevator went into high gear. We hit top speed a few seconds later and then the elevator started slowing down.

"We're running out of hose!" I said.

The elevator came to a complete stop, but we'd arrived where I could see about half the door to the kitchen. "We're not going to make it!"

But Floyd looked determined. He wasn't going to give up on my amazing plan. He untied the hose and wrapped it around himself five times, which made him look like some kind of hose mummy.

I stood back while Floyd started shaking and spinning like the Tasmanian Devil. And he bounced off the walls again. Then he shot through the gap into the kitchen like he was being blown out of a cannon. The hose stretched and stretched and stretched like an old ladies' pair of nylons.

"I should probably get out of this elevator," I said.

I climbed up to the kitchen and followed the hose. It was as tight as a slingshot pulled all the way back and ready to fire, and I couldn't imagine how Floyd was holding it in place. When I arrived at the front door, he had stretched his puny legs as wide as they would go. One leg was on each side of the doorjamb and the rest of Floyd was a ball of green in the middle.

"Hold on, Floyd!" I said. "You can do it!"

He was shaking like a leaf in a windstorm as I peered outside and saw that Sammy had the end of the hose inside Franny's mouth.

I picked up the phone in the front room and dialed a secret number for the laboratory.

"GOoooOooOOoooOOooooooOOOOOO ooo!" I cried when my dad picked up.

"Proceeding with release," Dr. Fuzzwonker said.

I heard him slap his palm down on a button.

Then I heard a sound like a tidal wave of water somewhere far away.

pancake watermelon

And finally I felt the hose burst to life. It went from flat as a pancake to wide as a watermelon and Fuzzwonker Fizz blasted into Franny's mouth at twenty gallons per second.

"It's working!" Sammy said.

"Backfilling underway," my dad said. "Four hundred additional gallons going into production."

I ran outside with the phone still on my ear so I could see what was happening. Poor Floyd was barely holding on and Franny—wow, she was blowing up like a balloon.

"Five hundred gallons released," Dr. Fuzzwonker said.

Franny was already bigger than a Volkswagen Bug. She expanded like a blowfish.

"You can do this, Franny," Sammy said, and she pet Franny's fur.

"Eight hundred gallons deployed," Dr. Fuzzwonker said. "Nine hundred. One thousand!"

"Only four hundred more gallons, Franny," I said. "You're practically full."

I didn't want to say anything that might alarm Franny, but she was getting really big. Her arms and legs were like toothpicks stuck in a head of lettuce. She was taller than the house.

lettuce

127

"Fourteen hundred gallons released," Dr. Fuzzwonker said. "We've done it."

"Okay, Floyd, you can let go now," I said. I was about to go hang up the phone when Floyd let the hose loose and it ricocheted off the walls as it was pulled at lightning speed back down the elevator. On the way out the hose hit a lamp, the coffeemaker, and a vase. They all exploded on impact.

"Floyd? Sammy?" I asked. "Where is everybody?"

I hung up the phone and walked outside. Wow. Franny was gigantic.

"Up here," Sammy said. I looked up and saw Sammy and Floyd sitting on top of Franny.

"Come on down, guys. We need to get Franny to the Snood Candy Factory. Pronto."

Floyd bounced off the roof and landed on my shoulder and Sammy slid down the side of Franny. We all stared at Franny's face. Her eyes were big and round, and it looked like she was holding her breath.

"You okay?" I asked.

Franny nodded very slowly, but I could tell we had to move fast. It was the dead of night in Pflugerville. The entire town was asleep, so at least we could move without being seen.

If we didn't get Franny to the Snoods quick, she was going to unleash one thousand four hundred gallons of Fuzzwonker Fizz in the middle of town.

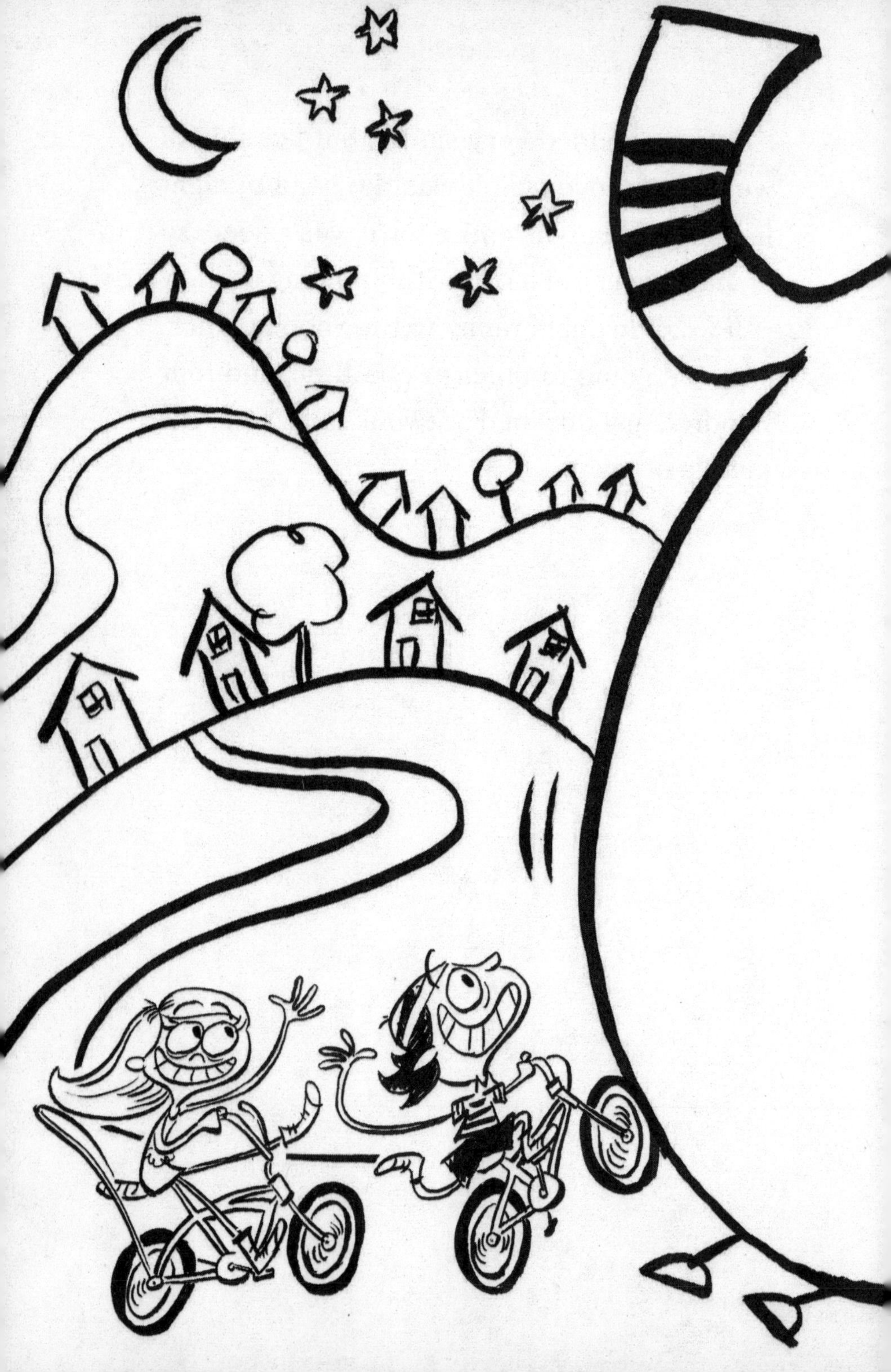

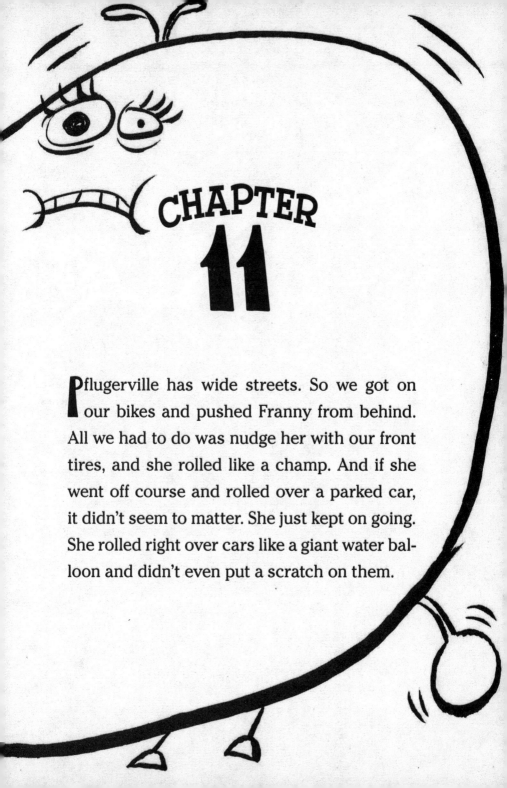

CHAPTER
11

Pflugerville has wide streets. So we got on our bikes and pushed Franny from behind. All we had to do was nudge her with our front tires, and she rolled like a champ. And if she went off course and rolled over a parked car, it didn't seem to matter. She just kept on going. She rolled right over cars like a giant water balloon and didn't even put a scratch on them.

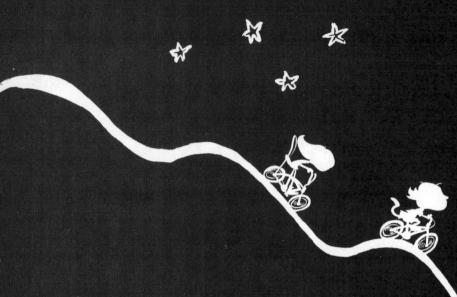

When we were going downhill, we picked up speed and rolled Franny into the uphill sections. Toward the end it was mostly uphill and that meant pushing Franny from behind with our bikes.

"I'm really glad we brought these specially designed Franny Movers," Sammy said as we gave it all we had. Franny Movers were just metal garbage can lids, but they helped a lot. We each lined up behind Franny on a different side of her and held the lids with one hand, pushing her up the hills. Her smooth fur crackled and popped as we went.

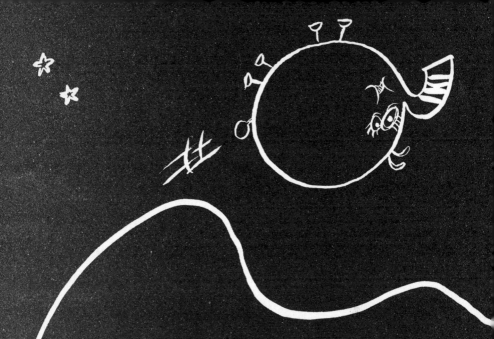

We rolled and rolled and rolled. Right past Sammy's house and on toward the bowling alley. It was so late no one was out driving around, and before we knew it, we'd pushed Franny all the way to Loopy Len's used car lot. When we got within a hundred feet of the covered bridge on the Snood property, we sped up and pushed her even harder. Then we veered off the driveway and gave her one last good shove. Franny rolled into the ravine and back up the other side, and then went airborne.

"Maybe that wasn't such a good idea," I said.

We dodged the Rambler and came out on the other side of the covered bridge, where Franny was bouncing like a basketball.

"She's heading for the Snood Candy Factory!" Sammy yelled.

Franny was spinning around and bouncing ten feet off the ground every time she landed, and I didn't know how we'd get her under control. But as usual, Floyd came to my rescue.

"Leave this to me," he said calmly into my ear. "You two get this door open."

Floyd jumped into the air, landed on the grass, and bounced all the way on top of Franny.

Sammy and I raced ahead on our bikes and dismounted at the door. When we looked back, Floyd was wrangling Franny like a cowboy, guiding her in our direction.

"She's coming in fast!" I said. "Throw open the door!"

Sammy and I both took hold of the big heavy door and opened it as wide as it would go.

It was still Floozombie madness inside. They'd dumped out the Snood's Flooze. They were wandering around like the undead Flooze monsters they were. Garvin was stuck to the wall next to his dad. There was Flooze plastered everywhere.

"Um, Harold?" Sammy said.

"Yeah?"

"I think we better get out of the way."

When I looked back outside I realized it was too late to do anything but enter the Snood Candy Factory. Franny was headed right for us, face-first.

We dove through the door and landed on slippery Flooze, sliding and rolling and getting completely covered from head to toe in Snood's disgusting candy. When we sat up, two Floozombies were standing right over us. They reached down with their green cheesy arms.

Franny hit the doorway and stuck like a cork. Her eyes darted back and forth until she saw me, and I nodded.

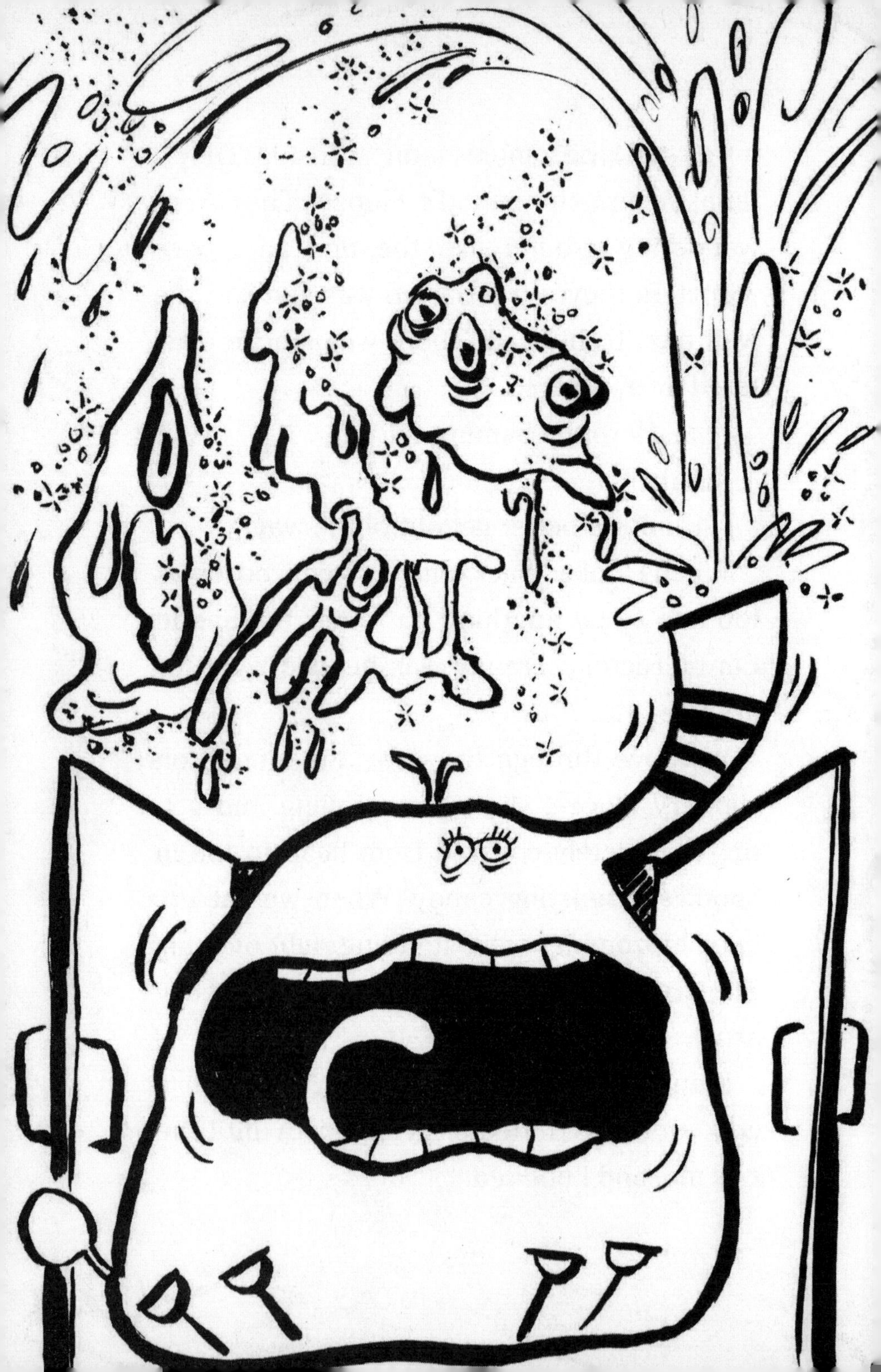

"She's gonna blow!" I said.

Sammy and I covered our heads and braced ourselves. Floyd leaped into my backpack. And then it happened.

Franny let out the biggest, longest, loudest burp in the history of biggest, longest, loudest burps. It was earth-shattering. The walls in the Snood Candy Factory shook. Fuzz-wonker Fizz blew out of Franny's mouth like water from a giant fire hose. The Floozombies were completely drenched. The whole place was! They slowly melted and fizzed and popped. Until finally they were just like the other Snood's Flooze that had poured out all over the factory.

Franny looked like someone who had just lost about ten thousand pounds. Her furry shell was stretched out, hanging in layers all around her.

"You did it, Franny!" I said.

"We should probably get out of here as fast as we can," Sammy said.

"Oh, right," I agreed. The Snoods had slid

down off the wall, and they were looking around like they had no idea what had just happened.

We made a break for it, covered in Snood's Flooze and Fuzzwonker Fizz.

"Come back here!" Mr. Snood yelled, but he was clearly confused. "Fuzzwonkeeeeeeeeeeeer!"

We were on our bikes and racing for home. Franny was all folded up into rolls so she could ride on Sammy's handlebars, and her furry coat was shrinking back to its normal size.

"You guys, that was the most amazing adventure we've ever had," Sammy said.

"And we saved Pflugerville from an invasion of Floozombies," I said.

"And Fizzopolis is still safely hidden from the Snoods," Sammy said.

There was only one thing left to do before the night was over. I called Floyd and Grabstack out of my backpack, and they both peeked out.

"You guys ready to put on a play or what?" I asked.

HAHA

HAHA

CHAPTER
12

BUUUURRP

Every Fizzy in Fizzopolis helped build a puppet theater stage at the edge of the lagoon. It was about ten feet wide and stood on four stilts. A red curtain covered the small stage where the show would come to life. The lights were dimmed to a twinkling purple hue as everyone settled in for the show. There were a hundred or more Fizzies eating popcorn and drinking Fuzzwonker Fizz. I sat in the front row with Sammy on one side and Franny on the other as a chorus of burping and laughter swept over the assembled crowd.

BUURRRP

HA HA

"I bet Grabstack and Floyd are nervous," Sammy said. "I hope they aren't back there throwing up."

I looked around Fizzopolis and thought about what a weird and wonderful place it was as the lights went down on the stage and a hush fell over the world of Fizzopolis. A single light illuminated a round spot in front of the puppet theater, and I stood up. When I was standing alone in the circle of light, I opened my arms as wide as they would go.

"Tonight was a really impressive team effort. Every Fizzy in Fizzopolis helped save the world from Floozombies. Give yourselves a fizzy round of applause!"

All the Fizzies started popping and fizzing. It sounded like a million pieces of bacon frying on a pan the size of a football field.

I quieted everyone down and called Franny and Sammy to stand with me. "And let's hear it for the big heroes of the day, Sammy, Franny, Floyd, and Dr. Fuzzwonker!"

Floyd peeked out from behind the red

Stadium

curtain and smiled like a goofball, and the crowd went wild. My dad waved from the back row in his white lab coat and nodded at everyone.

"And Harold Fuzzwonker!" Sammy yelled over the cheers.

The crowd fizzed even louder and threw popcorn at the stage until it felt like I was in a winter snowstorm.

"If everyone would please silence their cell

142

phones and stop drinking Fuzzwonker Fizz, I know the actors will appreciate it. No more burping until the show is over."

There were a few more random burps and then all was a hush as I left the spotlight and the curtain was drawn. Only Grabstack was there, all alone. He stared at his three feet for a moment and cleared his throat.

"Thank you all for being here tonight for the first ever showing of an original play entitled *The Mysterious Adventures of Mr. Pencil.* I will be assisted by Floyd."

All the Fizzies fizzed and popped with excitement. Grabstack looked right at me and mouthed two words that told me he had probably learned his lesson: *thank you.*

I smiled. If I could teach Grabstack to be a better Fizzy, anything was possible.

"On with the show!" Grabstack yelled, and then he was gone in a flash at stage left.

What followed was an epic tale of good versus evil that had the crowd on pins and needles. Dime and Penny were spun and rolled into our imaginations. Miss Ball of Rubber Bands and Mr. Pencil stole our hearts. The evil Floozemeister was replaced by the duo of Wrinkles, who used to be a grape, and the evil Mr. Lint Ball, and they were great villains.

When it was over, all the Fizzies in Fizzopolis gave Floyd and Grabstack a standing ovation full of burps and fizz and flying popcorn.

"We can never let the Snoods find out about Fizzopolis," Sammy said as she beamed from ear to ear.

And she was right. Fizzopolis really was the best place ever. After everything that had happened with the Floozombies, the Snoods would be more curious than ever. They'd stop at nothing to discover the secret of Fuzzwonker Fizz. But I had my best good buddy Floyd and my super-duper palamino Sammy to help me. The Floozombie outbreak taught me one thing for sure: Together, we could save Fizzopolis from anyone. Even a little blowhard like Grabstack!

THE END

Turn the page
for a sneak peek at

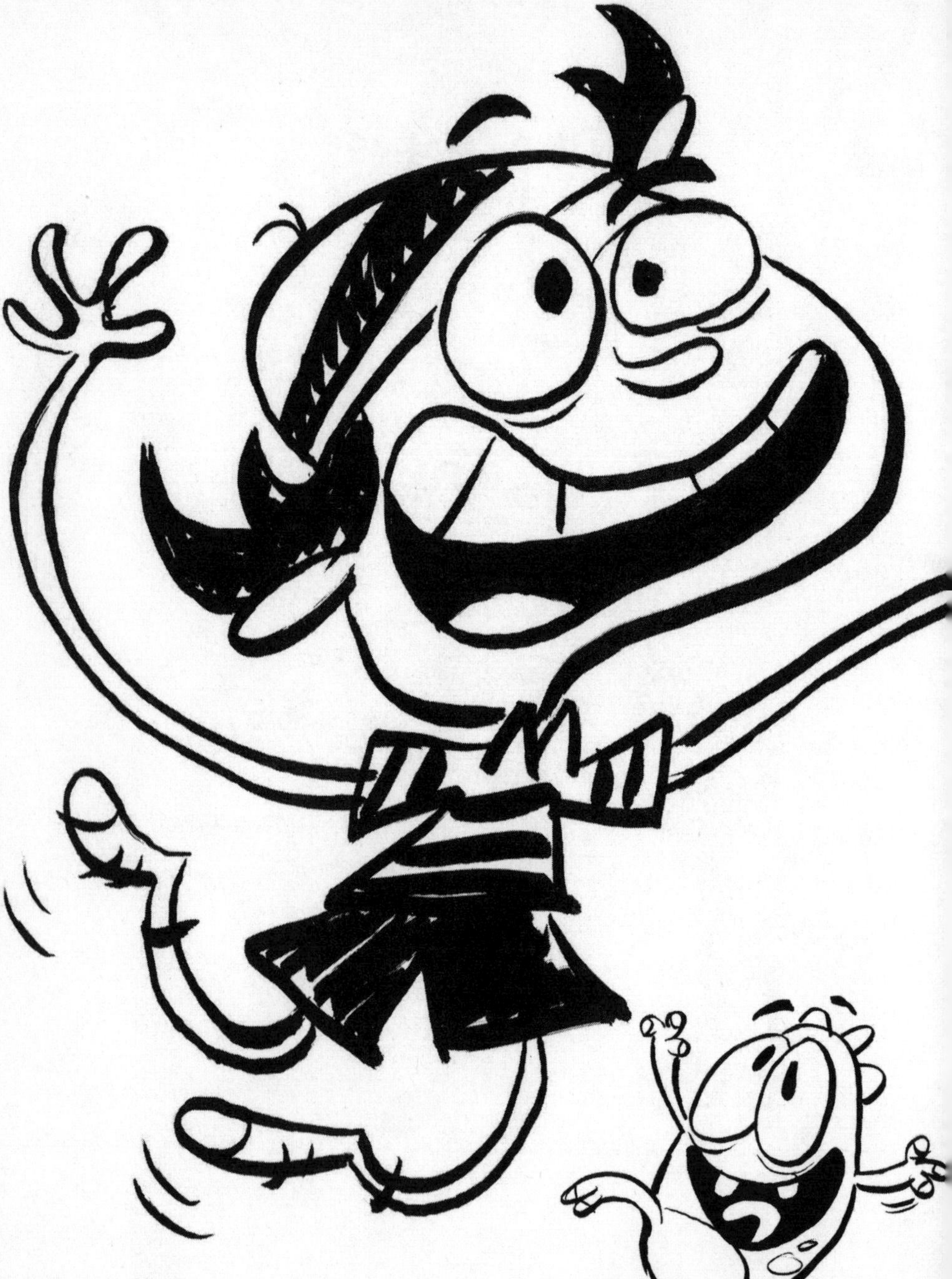

SUMMER VACATION CHAPTER 1

Hi, I'm Harold Fuzzwonker, and today I'm visiting Fizzopolis at ten o'clock on a Monday morning. Why, you might ask, am I not at school on this fine Monday morning? Why am I walking past the Fizzopolis lagoon instead of working on some math problems for my teacher, Miss Yoobler?

Because it's SUMMER VACATION! No classes! No homework! No Miss Yoobler! And most important, no Garvin Snood watching my every move in class. Let me repeat, IT'S SUMMER VACATION! Okay, so obviously I'm

1

excited, and when I get VERY excited,
I use ALL CAPS.

"Why is everybody meeting over
there?" I asked. Floyd, my best good
buddy, was sitting on my shoulder munching
on a hunk of cheddar cheese. He cheese-
mouth-mumbled something in my ear, but I
understood him.

"I agree," I said as we passed the Ping-Pong
table. "Let's go check it out. Whatever it is, it
must be important. And if it's important, we
need to know about it."

Floyd told me I was right, and added that
we practically ran the whole place, so why
weren't we invited to this important gather-
ing of Fizzies?

To say that we run the whole place might
be a slight exaggeration. My dad, Dr. Fuzzwonker, actually runs Fizzopolis. Most of the
time Floyd and I go to school and help out in
the afternoons with Fizzy chores.

"Hey, everybody!" I yelled as I approached
the gaggle of Fizzies. Nobody turned around.

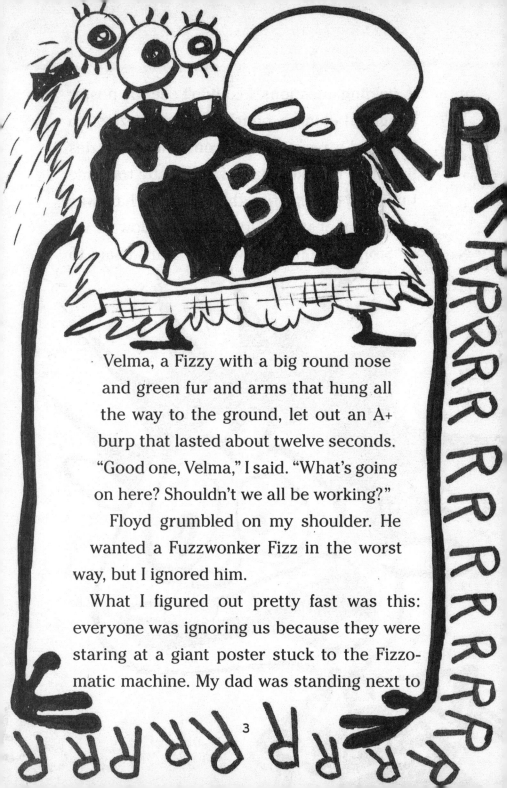

Velma, a Fizzy with a big round nose and green fur and arms that hung all the way to the ground, let out an A+ burp that lasted about twelve seconds. "Good one, Velma," I said. "What's going on here? Shouldn't we all be working?"

Floyd grumbled on my shoulder. He wanted a Fuzzwonker Fizz in the worst way, but I ignored him.

What I figured out pretty fast was this: everyone was ignoring us because they were staring at a giant poster stuck to the Fizzo-matic machine. My dad was standing next to

3

it, fielding questions. I couldn't see the poster hanging behind a bunch of furry Fizzies, so I pushed my way to the front. All the Fizzies fizzed as I walked past them, so by the time I popped out on the other side, my hair was totally full of static. I looked like a clown.

"Stop laughing at my weird hair," I said to Floyd.

4

I stared up at that sign and as I read it, the big fat grin on my face got bigger and bigger. This is what it said:

FIZZIES VS. FOOD COMPETITION!
10 MINUTES TO COOK, FLIP,
AND EAT PANCAKES
Each team will be comprised of
one cooker/flipper and one eater
THE TEAM THAT EATS
THE MOST PANCAKES WINS!
SIGN UP YOUR TEAM NOW
FIZZY VS. FOOD WILL TAKE PLACE
IN ONE WEEK
WINNERS RECEIVE:
1. Fame!
2. A full stomach!
3. A custom Fuzzwonker Fizz flavor of your choice!
4. Fame!

"Floyd!" I yelled. "We could totally win this thing. Look at all that fame we'd get! And we could come up with our own flavor!"

Floyd was nodding like a lunatic. My best good *eating* buddy was on board.

"Are there any more questions?" Dr. Fuzzwonker asked. He was standing in a white lab coat holding a clipboard and a pen.

That little blowhard Grabstack raised his paw and stepped forward like he owned the place. "Could you offer a tad more fame?"

"I'm glad you asked, Grabstack," my dad said. "I'm afraid I cannot offer any more fame. There's no more room on the poster."

Grabstack looked at the poster and nodded as if he understood.

"If that's all the questions," my dad said, "let's get back to work so we can finish for the day. Then there'll be more time to practice for the contest!"

My dad pulled me aside as all the Fizzies hustled back to their jobs.

"You and Floyd should take the next week

off. Consider it your paid summer vacation. Every kid needs a break."

I was thankful for the offer, but I knew my dad was giving us time off for a very different reason.

"You'd like to keep Floyd out of Fizzopolis for a week, wouldn't you?" I asked.

Floyd was high maintenance. He was always getting into mischief in Fizzopolis and making a lot of messes.

My dad tried to cover. "Who, him?" He pointed at Floyd. "Why would you say such a thing? We all love having Floyd around as much as possible."

My dad winked about nine times at me, so I got the idea. It wasn't me that needed a break from working in Fizzopolis. It was my dad who needed a break from Floyd!

"And just think, you could use this time to practice for FIZZIES VS. FOOD. You might even win!"

All that fame and our very own flavor of Fuzzwonker Fizz.

"You got a deal, Dad," I said. "We'll take the vacation."

As we headed for the elevator, I heard my dad sigh happily, like he was about to enter a day spa and have his toes manicured. I had it all figured out.

I would cook and flip, Floyd would eat and eat and eat. We'd have to be in perfect sync if we're going to win, and that meant practice, practice, practice.

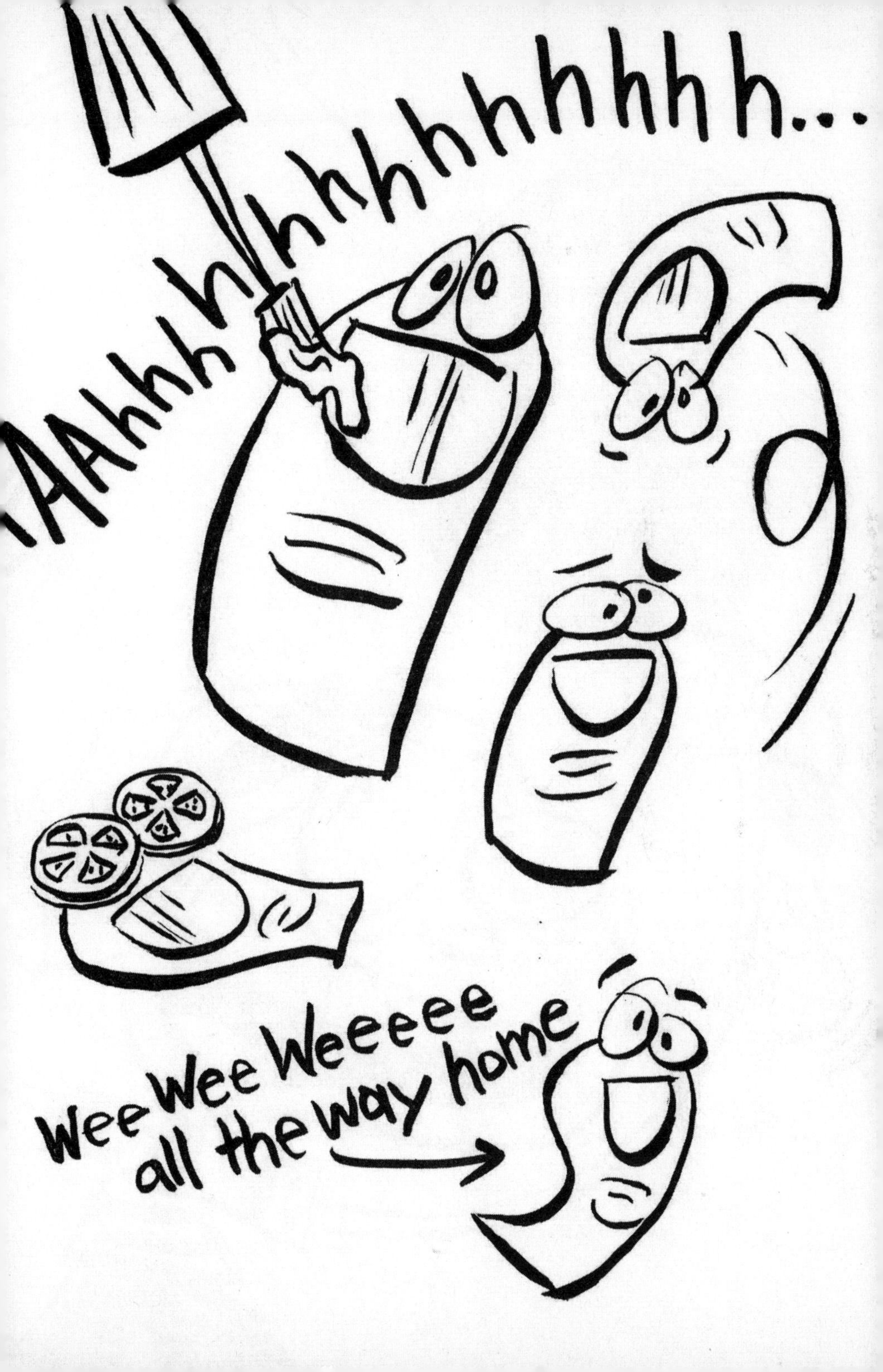
AAhhhhhhhhhhhhhhh...
Wee Wee Weeeee
all the way home

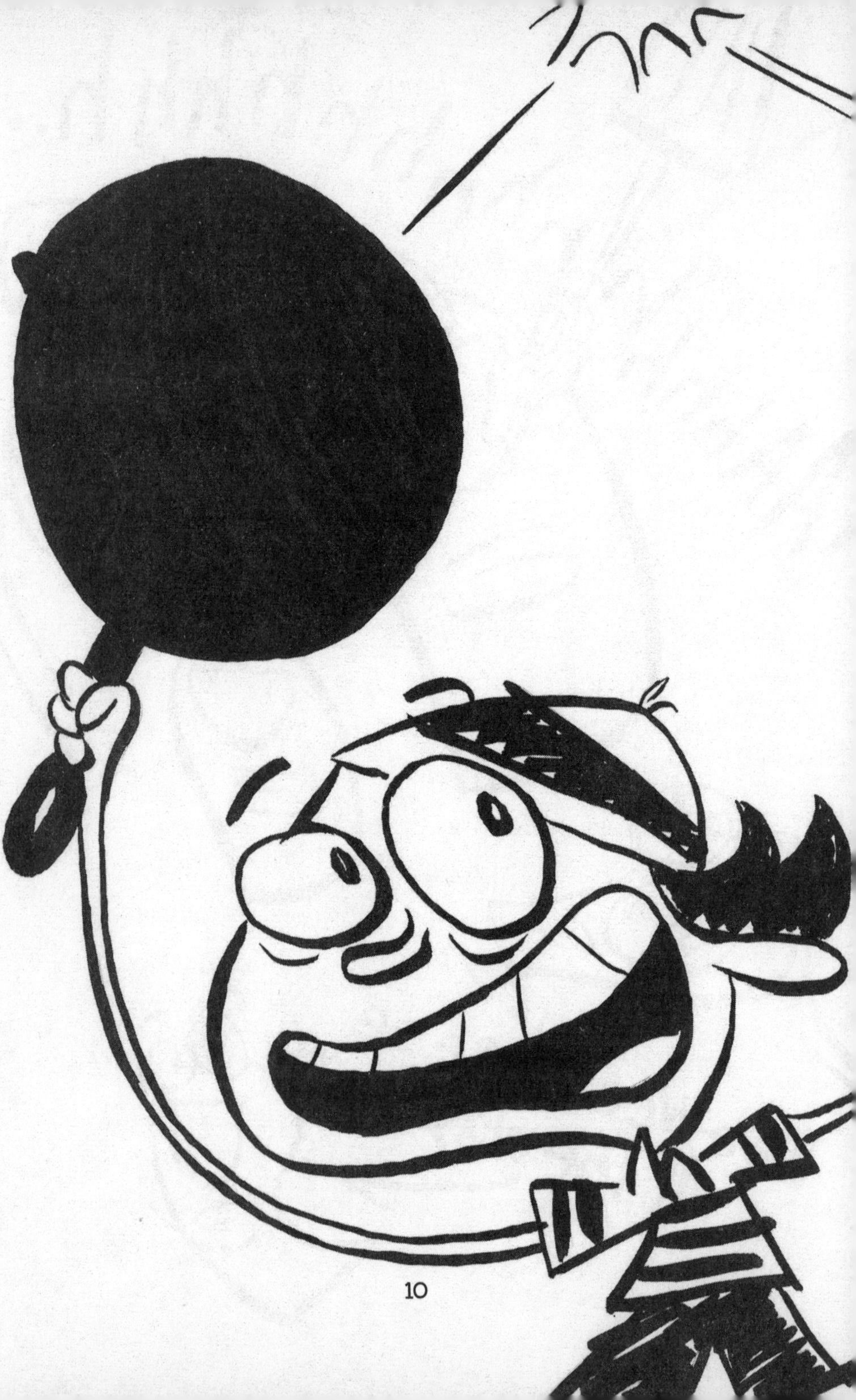

CHAPTER 2

"**N**umber one sixteen, coming up!" I yelled. I flipped the pancake over my head and it bounced off the ceiling, took a nosedive, and landed in Floyd's open mouth. It was his 116th pancake in fourteen minutes.

Floyd made a bunch of *munch munch munch* sounds and pounded his chest with his tiny fists. "Hit me again!" he yelled. When Floyd yells and he's not sitting on my shoulder with his head right next to my ear, it's hard to hear him. He has a very small voice, like what you might imagine a mouse would sound like if it could yell at you. Floyd made some more *munch munch munch* sounds, and I poured six more flapjacks onto the griddle. Fizzies vs. Food was only a week away, and Floyd would be going up against stiff competition. There would be tons of other Fizzies competing, and they were all a lot bigger than Floyd.

I turned around and looked at my best good buddy.

"How are you holding up?" I asked. We were hoping to get Floyd up to 150 in ten minutes. We were way short.

Floyd wobbled back and forth like he was going to pass out, then he pulled his tongue out of his head with his paw. It was dry as a bone.

"You must be parched," I said. "Let's call it a day and go work on the landing area for my jump over the house."

Floyd's tongue was lying on the counter like a piece of dried leather. The poor little dude was thirsty. Seriously, 116 pancakes will do that to a guy. I went to the refrigerator and searched for a bottle of Fuzzwonker Fizz. I looked behind a head of cabbage, but there was none there. I peeked behind the eggs and the cheese and inside the fruit crisper. No Fuzzwonker Fizz.

"That's weird," I said, scratching my head. "We've never, ever, in the history of ever, run out of Fuzzwonker Fizz."

Floyd waddled over with his gut sticking out and his tongue dragging behind him.

He jumped on my shoulder and his tongue slapped me in the back of the head.

"Could you put that thing back in your mouth?" I said. "It's gross. And dangerous."

Floyd pointed to a gallon of milk in the fridge and practically broke my eardrum. "MIIIIIIILLLLLLLLLK!"

"I wish I could give you a Fuzzwonker Fizz," I said. "In a pinch, milk will have to do."

I uncorked the milk jug and leaned the opening toward Floyd. He opened his mouth about as wide as a manhole cover and I poured the entire gallon in there. I don't know where he puts this stuff.

He burped. Milk burps are generally lame compared to Fuzzwonker Fizz burps, and this one was no exception.

Floyd asked if he could use the bathroom.

"By all means, please do," I said.

While Floyd was gone I turned off the griddle and stacked up the six pancakes he hadn't eaten. I held them like a sandwich and started munching while I took one last look inside the refrigerator for a bottle of Fuzzwonker Fizz.

Not a single bottle in there.

By the time Floyd got back I was as thirsty as he was, but he'd guzzled down all the milk. I slurped a warm glass of water from the tap and nearly barfed all over the kitchen floor.

"We need Fuzzwonker Fizz in the worst way," I said. I thought that if we went down into Fizzopolis, my dad might put us to work and cut our vacation short. "Let's go see if Sammy has any we can borrow."

Floyd is my best good buddy, and Sammy is my super-duper palomino. It's good to have both if you can get them, just in case one is out of town or has the flu or falls into a hole or something.

"Let's go set up my next world-famous Pflugerville bike jump. We can do some practice jumps on the way," I said as I mounted my red bike. I didn't need to carry my books around in the summer, so instead I used this nifty fanny pack I found at a garage sale. Floyd fit in there perfectly, and it was a lot lighter to carry him around. Plus, he could be right up front and open the zipper so he could see what was going on.

On the way to Sammy's I jumped over seven different things, in the following order:

A poodle.

An oscillating sprinkler.

A yard gnome.

A paper bag (we went back and picked it up and put it in a trash can).

A trash can (the one we put the bag in!).

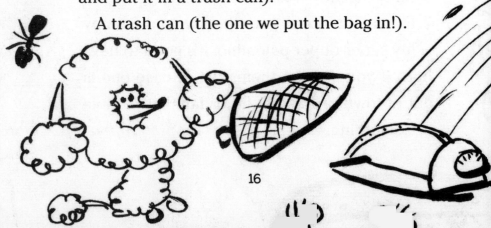

An anthill
(no ants were harmed in
the making of that jump).
And a pinecone.

We tried to jump over a cat sleeping on the sidewalk, but it woke up and ran away before we could get there. Cats are hard to jump over because they're so skittish.

By the time we got to Sammy's front door, I was even thirstier than I'd been back at the house. We walked up to the front door, but before I could knock, Sammy jumped out from behind a bush and pushed me into the yard. I landed on my butt.

"Gotcha!" she yelled, and then she ran away.

I stood up and Floyd jumped up on my shoulder. There was no one around, so I didn't make him get back in the fanny pack. We waited about ten seconds and Sammy came running around the other side of her house. She was really moving, but we hadn't chased her, so she basically ran right into us.

I tagged her on the shoulder.

"Good strategy you got there," she said. "But after you tag me you're supposed to run away. That's how the game works."

"Actually, if we could play this later, we're

searching for a bottle of Fuzzwonker Fizz," I said. "We might die of thirst right here on your lawn if we don't get one soon."

"Come to think of it, I'm thirsty, too," Sammy said. She was out of breath from all that running. "Let's see what flavors I have. Come on."

Floyd got back inside the fanny pack, just in case Sammy's mom or dad or the little bundle of baby they had in there was awake.

"How's your little brother doing?" I asked. Her brother, Owen, wasn't even a year old.

"He tried to eat a paper cup yesterday," she said. "I don't think he's all that bright. But I like him. He cracks me up."

We arrived at the fridge and she pulled the door open. There was a bowl of potato salad in there and Floyd jumped out of my fanny pack and started attacking it.

"He just ate one hundred and sixteen pancakes," I said. "He's like a garbage disposal."

Sammy and I rummaged through her refrigerator. We explored behind the leftovers and the orange juice and the ham.

"Looks like we're out," she said, peering inside one more time. "Come to think of it, I haven't had a Fuzzwonker Fizz in days."

I just knew something was fishy. And when something's fishy, usually the Snoods are involved.

"Come on, you guys," I said. "Let's go check the Pflugermart. There's got to be some Fuzzwonker Fizz there."

We took off on our bikes and headed for the supermarket in Pflugerville. I hardly spoke at all while we pedaled as fast as we could.

Why wasn't there any Fuzzwonker Fizz at my house or Sammy's?

Something was definitely, positively, for sure fishy!

About the Author and Artist

PATRICK CARMAN is the *New York Times* best-selling author of the acclaimed series Land of Elyon and Atherton and the teen superhero novel *Thirteen Days to Midnight*. A multimedia pioneer, Patrick authored *The Black Circle*, the fifth title in the 39 Clues series, and the ground-breaking Dark Eden, Skeleton Creek, and Trackers series. An enthusiastic reading advocate, Patrick has visited more than a thousand schools, developed village library projects in Central America, and created author outreach programs for communities. He lives in Walla Walla, Washington, with his family. You can visit him online at www.patrickcarman.com.

BRIAN SHEESLEY is a five-time Emmy Award–winning director, animator, and designer of some of the most popular animated cartoon shows ever, including *Futurama*; *Camp Lazlo!*; *King of the Hill*; *Fanboy and Chum Chum*; *Regular Show*; and *The Simpsons*. He lives in Los Angeles, California, with his family.

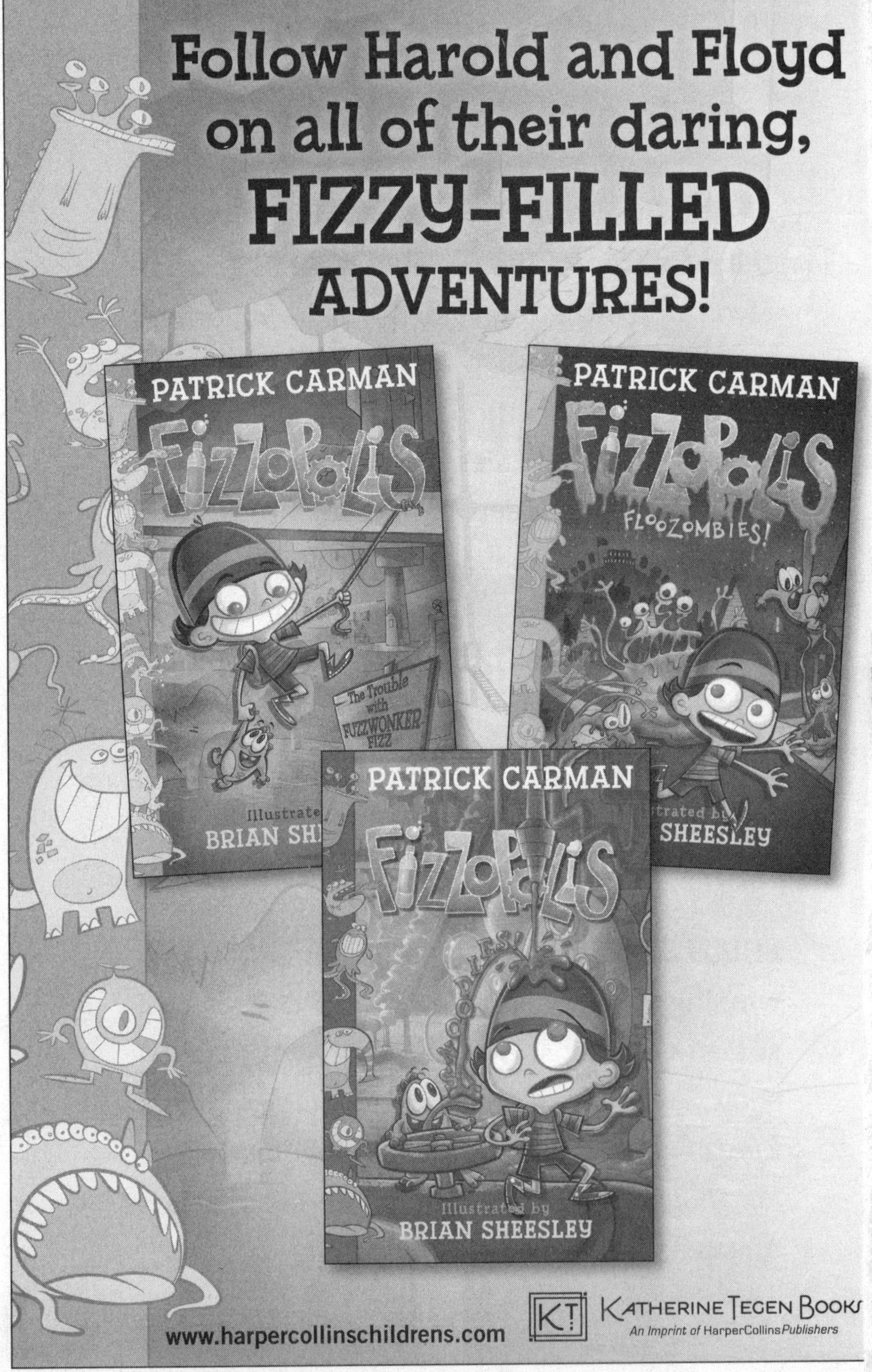
Follow Harold and Floyd
on all of their daring,
FIZZY-FILLED
ADVENTURES!
PATRICK CARMAN
FIZZOPOLIS
The Trouble with FUZZWONKER FIZZ
Illustrate
BRIAN SH
PATRICK CARMAN
FIZZOPOLIS
FLOOZOMBIES!
strated by
SHEESLEY
PATRICK CARMAN
FIZZOPOLIS
Illustrated by
BRIAN SHEESLEY
www.harpercollinschildrens.com
KT
KATHERINE TEGEN BOOKS
An Imprint of HarperCollinsPublishers